# THE
# Beduins' Gazelle

A RICHARD JACKSON BOOK

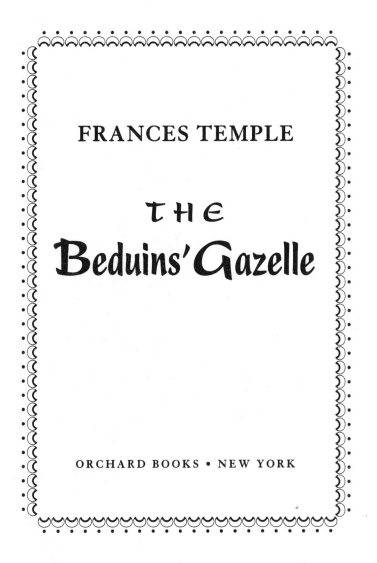

FRANCES TEMPLE

# THE
# Beduins' Gazelle

ORCHARD BOOKS • NEW YORK

Orchard Books, 95 Madison Avenue, New York, NY 10016

Manufactured in the United States of America
Book design by Mina Greenstein
The text of this book is set in 12 point Granjon.

2  4  6  8  10  9  7  5  3  1

Library of Congress Cataloging-in-Publication Data
Temple, Frances.
The Beduins' gazelle / by Frances Temple.   p.   cm.
"A Richard Jackson book"—Half t.p.
Sequel to: The Ramsay scallop.
Summary: In 1302, two cousins of the nomadic Beni Khalid tribe
who are betrothed become separated by political intrigue between
warring tribes.
ISBN 0-531-09519-3.   ISBN 0-531-08869-3 (lib. bdg.)
[1. Bedouins—Fiction.   2. Deserts—Fiction.   3. Middle East—
Fiction.]   I. Title.
PZ7.T244Be   1996   [Fic]—dc20   95-33530

*Frances finished this book on her last day with us. A heart attack, rare and sudden as a lightning bolt from a sunny sky, struck her while we walked our dog along Seneca Lake. "Tell me nice things," she said, as the feeling took hold of her. Then she laid her head in my lap and died.*

*I know she would have wanted to thank Dick Jackson for hearing what she had to say, and for guiding her through all six of her books; Maggie Herold, Amy Kaufman, and the other wonderful people at Orchard Books; and Ginee Seo, her editor at Harper Trophy. She would have wanted to thank the people at Children's Literature of New England for their support; the Women's International Foundation for Peace and Freedom, for their honor of the Jane Addams Children's Book Award; her many fine and careful reviewers; Milagros Rosario for stories that found their way into* Taste of Salt; *Ivon, Hugo, and Veronica for letting her tell* Grab Hands and Run; *her sister Lindsay for stories and companionship as she researched* The Ramsay Scallop; *the Washington Office on Haiti, Rosemarie Cierici, and Edwidge Danticott for many details that went into* Tonight, by Sea.

*Perhaps she is even now thanking her late father, Ambassador Frederick Nolting, for taking her away to see the world at an early age and for sharing his concern for humanity, his lively curiosity, and his unshakable moral courage. She would certainly have wished to thank her mother, Lindsay, for love and language and her sisters, Molly, Lindsay, and Jane, for lively companionship. She has left a legacy of love, energy, and stories with her daughters, Anna Brooke, Jessie, and Tyler— and with scores of her students at the Children's Hours School—and with me.*

CHARLES TEMPLE
*Geneva, New York*
*October 2, 1995*

# CONTENTS

*The year in which this story takes place is*
*680 of the Hegira according to the*
*Muslim calendar, and, according*
*to the Christian calendar, the*
*year of our Lord 1302.*

# There Was, There Was Not . . .

Halima sat with her chin resting on her knees, close enough to touch her kinspeople, yet with her mind far away. The singsong of the storyteller's voice lulled her. The lanterns threw a soft glow on the dark wall of the tent, on the red and brown embroidered cushions, on the familiar faces of the listening women and children. Halima played with her ankle bangles, her mind drifting with the story.

"There was, there was not, in the oldness of time . . ."

The wind sighed outside the tent, blowing the desert sand across the infinite spaces of the great sand sea, lifting it in swirls, buffeting the tent sides. Inside, Halima smiled in the shadows, resting her forehead on her knees.

Through every long day, Halima tried not to

dream. People in the camp said that only a fool or a donkey let their steps be guided by love. Every Khalidi woman knew it was shameful to show what was in your heart, even toward the boy to whom you were promised from birth, your own cousin. "Girls who dream lose their strength, forget how to cook, drop their water jars," her mother, Miriam, had warned her just this morning, on the way to the well.

And it was true, of course.

But that was in daytime.

Story time was different. No one could see her face or read her heart. She could think whatever she wanted. Enfolded in darkness, Halima allowed herself glimpses of her cousin in her mind's eye—the arch of an eyebrow; the quick, clear glance as he asked a question; the sound of his laugh. As the stories of djinns and princesses loosed the thoughts of the women and children from their everyday worries, Halima dreamed of her cousin Atiyah, to whom she was promised, whose name meant the Gift of God.

Yawning, she pulled a big pillow to her and curled around it, its embroidery rough against her face. The pillow smelled like sheep and smoke. Halima sighed and closed her eyes, listening to the wind.

She woke with a jolt. The lantern was out, the storyteller gone. A hand was gripping her ankle, pulling hard.

"Halima, wake up. Cousin! I need to tell you something!"

Atiyah's voice.

Atiyah, here?! Anger swept Halima; her hair rose on her scalp like a jackal's. It was fine and wonderful to daydream of Atiyah in the privacy of the women's tent, in the hour set apart for stories. It made her furious to have him here now, shaking her foot in the dark. By what right was he so near her? Had he no respect?

"Go!" She pushed at him. He caught her hand, but she jerked it away. She was a Khalidi girl; if she and Atiyah were found alone together before marriage, she would be put to death, and rightly so, to protect the honor of the tribe. Halima imagined the cutlass's slice; the skin on her neck tingled. She kicked Atiyah, hard. "Go away!" she whispered. "Out!"

Atiyah rolled under the tent side, then stuck his head back into the tent and whispered, "Come on! Essafeh won't kill *you*, light of his heart, light of his eyes. . . ."

[3]

Halima shook her head in the dark and rubbed her bruised ankle. Atiyah understood nothing. If her father, Essafeh, caught her, he would have to kill her *because* he loved her. The rules that keep the tribe honorable are more important than a father's affection. As any fool should know.

Halima sat, her hands around her neck. "*Hamdillah* . . . ," she murmured, "the merciful, the compassionate . . ."

Then suddenly curiosity got the better of her, and she wriggled after her cousin. She came out beside him, tangled in her robe, where the side of the black felt tent sheltered them from the wind.

"*Majnun,*" she called him. "Madman! Why—?"

Atiyah's hands flew up in the dark, palms out, to fend off her anger. "Forgive me, Cousin! There was no other way. You may never see me again, not for years!" There was a flash of teeth.

Was Atiyah smiling?

"If you speak truth, you are too happy, Cousin," said Halima, wanting to twist his arm behind his back, wishing they could still fight like children. "Tell more."

"I've come to say good-bye. I've been sent away— banished!"

"After all these years, my parents have come to

their senses . . . ," Halima murmured between her teeth. She crossed her arms. "The reason, Atiyah?"

Atiyah glanced behind him. "Passing shepherds brought a rumor. There are wars in the north. The caliph wants men. . . ."

"You are not a man yet." She stopped. He was, almost.

Atiyah took no notice. "They say our uncle Saladeen has left the city of Fez and is riding toward our tents."

"And so Essafeh banishes you?"

"For my own safety. Essafeh trusts no one from the city, not even his own brother. He doesn't want Saladeen to find me here. Essafeh told me, 'Go, Atiyah. Go! Raid our enemies the Shummari or hunt lizards in the desert. Stay away, at least until the moon has waxed and waned again, until my brother Saladeen has left our tents.'"

"Until the moon has waxed and waned . . . ," Halima echoed. She could see Atiyah now in the faint starlight that filtered through the blowing dust. His head cloth was in his hand, his black hair clumped with sand. He turned so that they sat facing each other, both cross-legged, knees touching. Standing or sitting, they were of a height.

A moon or two. Halima's heart settled back in its

rightful place. Words came from a cool corner in her mind. "You have so little faith in me, Cousin, that a few moons apart should mean forever?" She was pleased by the smoothness of her words.

Atiyah rested his forehead against hers. His eyes were almond shaped. The white triangles at the corners flew this way and that as he spoke.

"Halima," he said, "in two moons, the rain clouds may roll into our sky and burst, and we Khalidi will dance in the desert among flowers."

"The people will throw water rings in the wadi," said Halima, falling into the game of poetry making.

"Our feet will scatter rainbows. . . ."

"Our fingers will gather tender thistle shoots. . . ."

"The voices of the Khalidi will sing with frogs. . . ." Halima sat back and wound a strand of hair around her finger, trying to think of another line. She was anxious for Atiyah, but even more, she was envious. He threw himself into danger like a hawk. He took joy in risk. Her worry, flung around him, would be cumbersome and boring as a blanket.

She wished Essafeh would send her away, too. "We will rise with the warm wind under our wings," she said, longing to be a hawk.

"I'm leaving," he said. "Now. The wind is blowing enough sand to cover my tracks."

Halima took his hands, feeling the bones, counting them. She touched his knuckles to her forehead.

"Go, then," she said, throwing his hands from her. "May Allah smooth your path homeward."

As if her words were magic, he rose and disappeared.

Halima sat alone, listening to the moan of the wind. She watched to see Atiyah ride off but saw only the skittish moon shadows of blown sand, moving like ghosts across the dunes, all flowing away from her. Tears stung her nose and eyes. She sat until the tears dried on her cheeks. She wiped her nose on the back of her hand, crawled into the tent, and slept.

# 2

# Banished

Atiyah settled into the swinging gallop of his camel, urging it along with a low-whistled song, alert to the changing sounds under its feet. Beneath the loose blowing sand he heard rock, shale, hard-packed sand. Sometimes his camel broke through a sand crust; it would sway sideways, then regain its balance by running even faster. Atiyah leaned forward, his chest against the beast's hump, his fingers locked in its hair, listening through its body for the sucking sounds that meant quicksand.

His excitement at being banished from Essafeh's camp was fading. He tried to revive it by glancing from the corners of his eyes at shadows, shaping them into monsters. That cave, for instance: Couldn't it be a *dhabi,* the mystery hyena who lures travelers to their deaths—the top of the shadow forming its rough-edged, flopped-over ear, that hole in the dark wall a gleaming eye? If Halima were with him, she would see it.

On foot, he might be attacked by a mountain lion. On camelback, he was disgustingly safe.

"Essafeh, Essafeh, why are you so concerned with *safety*?" Atiyah asked the moon.

Essafeh, his uncle and adoptive father, was the man Atiyah most wanted to be like.

It was said of Essafeh that his words were like milk, without fault. It was said that wherever he pointed his lance, his aim was always true. It was said that his hospitality was so great, the coffee grounds piled up before his tent like a mountain. Essafeh shouted with laughter when he heard these tales; Atiyah shared Essafeh's pride and delight when men flocked to follow him in a raid or followed his family into the deep desert to compete for the honor of pitching their tents near his. Essafeh was the leader the Beni Khalid had chosen, the one they followed joyfully. There was nothing in all the great harsh world of the desert that Essafeh feared, besides dishonor.

So why, Atiyah asked the moon, was Essafeh afraid of Saladeen?

Saladeen, Essafeh's brother, had left the desert

and taken up with the powerful city Arabs in Fez. He was a mullah, a teacher of Islamic faith. If the rumors were true, Saladeen had been sent to recruit warriors for a jihad: Saladeen claimed that jihads were holy wars, that their purpose was to convert the heathen to Islam. Essafeh said the wars were not holy at all, that their purpose was to increase the power of the caliph, who wanted to rule even the desert tribes. And that the desert tribes had always chosen, and would always choose, their own leaders and their own enemies.

Whenever Essafeh spoke of Saladeen, anger made his face dark as a plum and he moved unsteadily.

Atiyah was suspicious of Saladeen, but he was not afraid, and he would not have chosen to hide from him.

As for his real father, Atiyah could picture him only as he had once heard him described, dead in a pool of his own red blood, slain in a raid upon an enemy tribe.

Atiyah leaned back in his saddle, pushing against his stirrups, feeling the strength of his legs and back and neck. His real father had chosen his name, Atiyah, the Gift of God. His father must have noticed, in the few days he held and saw him, that his infant son was perfect.

Atiyah flicked the camel switch impatiently. He admired Essafeh. He loved Essafeh. But he was angry with him. Atiyah's distrust of Saladeen had an edge of pleasure to it: His suspicions made him sharp and cunning in a way he could never be with Essafeh.

How could Essafeh be so sure that Atiyah didn't want to fight in a jihad? He had never asked him, not once! Essafeh had sheltered and protected Atiyah all through his childhood, but Atiyah was no longer a child. Essafeh had no right to make all decisions for him.

Atiyah imagined himself galloping across the sands with a thousand warriors around him, each shouting his passionate soul up into the clear blue sky. . . . A war might be fun.

By the time he returned home to the black tents of Essafeh, he would be a man, and Halima would be a woman fully grown.

Atiyah wanted to return to camp, to hear what Saladeen had in mind.

A sudden crunch brought him back to reality. His camel faltered. Atiyah slid off quickly, to help his mount find its way across a patch of treacherous ground.

# 3

# Watched

U p, girl! We have guests coming!" The hand shaking Halima this time could only be her mother's. The tent side was rolled high. Sunlight poured in. The wind had died; the sky was clear blue. The sands glittered, traceless, warming fast.

The sudden crackle of burning thornbush, the slow warm smell of smoldering camel dung told Halima that someone else had lit the morning cook-fires and she had overslept. She hurried to make herself ready for the day, washing with the wet cloth her mother handed her. Wake-up sounds: the slapping of bread dough, the pounding of the coffee mortars. Her brothers, Yusef and Wahid, just younger than she and nearly as tall, made a dance of crushing freshly roasted beans in the mortar outside the tent, clacking the pestle against the inner rim of the mortar and then throwing it down with a crunch, releasing the sharp smell of coffee.

How could she have slept? Inside the tent, dark in contrast to the bright sand outside, copper pots hanging on the support poles caught the light and gleamed. From among the scattered pillows, the tousled heads of her smaller sisters rose like the sudden blooming of flowers after a desert rain. Goats bleated nearby, impatient to be milked. It was a morning like every morning.

Maybe I dreamed that Atiyah was banished, thought Halima. What could be dangerous about Saladeen? He is our uncle, and family is to be trusted.

But she looked in all his usual places, and Atiyah was nowhere to be seen. And her sleeping pallet was full of sand.

W hy must we feast Uncle Saladeen? *You* don't like him. *I* don't like him. He looks like the Father of Dung. So why must we feast him?" Halima's little sister Nazreen questioned her mother, Miriam, as the three of them stood together, Miriam combing and plaiting the little girl's long hair, Halima poking in a box, finding beads to adorn the ends of the braids. Halima knew what the answer would be before Miriam spoke.

"Everyone is someone, Nazreen. And we are the Beni Khalid. No one goes hungry from our tents."

Nazreen, keeping her head very still, scratched

her leg with one toe. "Saladeen minds, doesn't he, that Father is loved and called Essafeh the Welcomer, whereas he is called *City* Saladeen? Nobody likes him. It makes him angry with us, doesn't it, Mother?"

"Shhh, Nazreen. We will not speak ill of a guest and kinsman."

City Saladeen, thought Halima. Father of Dung. She gave one of Nazreen's braids a tug, wishing she herself could still get away with such questions.

Halima was out milking the goats when Saladeen and his men came into sight over the crest of a dune. She jumped to her feet to watch their arrival. The newcomers' white robes sparkled against the blue sky; their head cloths snapped in the breeze like banners. Men hurried out to greet them, goatskins of precious well water slapping against their knees. Atiyah was not among them.

Halima knelt and stripped the last rich milk from a goat's udder, then patted the goat roughly on her bony rump, rose, and moved on to the next.

Behind the tents, her brothers were digging a roasting pit big enough for a camel. Among their shouts, she heard the camel's sudden, loud death cry: The men and boys had slit its throat to prepare Saladeen's welcome feast.

Halima stopped milking, her hands still around the goat's teats, and rested her head on the animal's flank. She should feel proud that her father could honor a guest with a whole camel. Its flesh would be eaten. Its hair would go to make the black tents of Essafeh bigger. Yet she had seen that camel drooping its eyelid above the campfire, smiling at the stories, and now it had been turned to mere meat and cloth with the thrust of a knife.

Stroking the goat's bag to bring down the milk, Halima tried to shrug away the question slaughter always raised: Where did the life go? Could this happen to her? To Atiyah?

If only she were with him, wherever he was. Atiyah had no fear of death and would chase her dread with jokes.

The bright sun warm on her neck, Halima shivered.

*Cha-aa!* I'm worse than a baby! she told herself, finishing the last goat and slapping her rump to send her on her way. As she stood, words to a song Atiyah sang at every opportunity came to mind: "Tall as sugarcane and as sweet . . ." Her arms shaking, Halima carefully lifted the bowl full of milk to her head. She settled the bowl on her head cloth and, steadying it lightly with her fingertips, walked with careful smoothness back toward the women's tent.

Halfway from the goat pen to the center of camp, she passed the guest tent—and suddenly felt watched. A little shiver of shame and pride ran up her back. She glided past, looking straight ahead, neither hurrying nor slowing.

Outside the *zenana,* she helped her mother scour the long metal platters with sand, so that they would shine for the feast. She set some milk in the sun to sour, and some she mixed with dried dates to sweeten it for drinking, then put it in the shade to cool. She took down the copper bowls from the tent posts and filled them with dried dates and nuts from the storage sacks.

Summoned to the greeting tent, Halima stood before her father and uncle, holding Nazreen's hand. Yusuf and Wahid stood on either side of them; Layla and Aleya clutched her skirt. Halima greeted her uncle and after one quick glance into his face, lowered her gaze to his braided sandals.

"Last year, she was a loudmouthed child. Now she is like a gazelle caught before the hunter," Saladeen said. "My beautiful niece Halima, betrothed to my nephew Atiyah, the Gift of God. . . . "

Saladeen ran the side of his finger along Halima's cheek, from ear to chin. Halima's skin flinched—he treats me like an eggplant from the oasis, she thought, whose flaws he will point out to save barter. She raised her head, looking away from him.

"You are to be proud, my brother," Saladeen concluded.

Halima's father, Essafeh, nodded politely.

"And the noble Atiyah himself, why has he not come to greet his uncle?"

"Atiyah is searching for missing stock. He left just before your messenger came to us," Essafeh answered.

*"Ah-ahh!"* growled Saladeen. "Another raid!"

Nazreen clutched Halima's hand more tightly. Halima felt her eyes open wide. Saladeen's mood change was like a freak storm, arisen suddenly, without warning.

Why should her uncle scorn them?

What did he want from Atiyah?

Halima reminded herself that women of the Beni Khalid worked, kept their counsel, and did not question men.

Outwardly calm, straight as sugarcane, Halima held up the kettle of water and hand cloth, so that their guest could wash before eating.

[ 17 ]

# 4

# Captured

By high noon Atiyah had reached the Wadi el-Djemar, where a seasonal stream had cut a path through sandstone, a crevasse deep enough to paint a zigzag of shadow. Atiyah jumped from his camel into its shade, whipped off his head cloth, shook his hair into a black bush around his head, and took a deep breath of the cool air. Then he hobbled his mount, singing soothing words to it as he crawled beneath its legs:

> *"Forgive this indignity,*
> *Beautiful camel.*
> *I'm tying your feet,*
> *Your wand'ring to . . . to . . ."*

Atiyah pressed the back of his hand against the camel's neck, and it sank to its knees.

> *" . . . Trammel!* Trrammel!"

Atiyah savored the rhyme. He began to sing again, stroking the camel's neck as it closed its heavy-lidded eyes:

> *"Dream quietly of traveling,*
> *Beautiful camel.*
> *I've hobbled your legs,*
> *Your wand'ring to trammel.*

"Brilliant Atiyah!" he added. He stood and stretched his arms to the side, his fists clenched. He danced in a tight circle, dipping and turning like a falcon at the top of its climb, humming, his eyes closed. He felt sun and shade flicker on his face as he turned, and the next verse came to him:

> *"Shade-giving wadi,*
> *Shelter our flight,*
> *Deep desert cove*
> *Of . . . blah-blah-blah light.*
> *Lavender light?*
> *Cool, pearly light . . .*
> *Deep desert cove*
> *Of cool, pearly light."*

The camel wove its head back and forth, eyes shut, nostrils distended.

Atiyah stretched out on his back on the soft sand

at the bottom of the wadi, wriggled to make himself comfortable, and closed his eyes.

He woke feeling thuds through the sand. Horses. In one silent motion, he rolled over and stood. The crevasse was all shadow now. He stuck his head up. Two men were approaching on horseback. Narrowing his eyes to make them out, Atiyah recognized distant cousins who now followed Saladeen. He remembered them as boys—Hassan and Ahmed, were they?—always together, slow in speech. They had grown very large.

Atiyah stopped squinting and waved his head cloth.

"My kinsmen!" he called to them cheerfully. "Welcome! Hassan! Ahmed! The sight of you lights my evening. Have you come to accompany me on a raid, to help me increase the glory and wealth of the Beni Khalid? A thousand moons have waxed and waned since we last rode together, Cousins. Your company will be welcome."

The two large cousins looked at Atiyah, their mouths hanging open.

"May Allah bless—," Hassan began.

"Health to the brave," Ahmed muttered simultaneously.

The brothers exchanged a scowl. Hassan made a cutting motion with his hand to silence Ahmed.

"Saladeen wants to see you and tells you to tell us—I mean tells us to tell you. . . . He says stop your raid and come greet him in the tent of—you know—the other brother—Essafeh," he said, all in a rush, then cleared his throat, spat, and looked triumphantly at his brother.

"Right. He said to grab you fast," added Ahmed.

Clever Saladeen, thought Atiyah, to give such dolts employment, and to catch me in a web of family obligation.

To allow Hassan and Ahmed their triumph, he pretended disappointment. "Come, Cousins." Sighing deeply, he turned to unstrap a packet of figs from his saddlebag. "We will eat together in the shade the wadi grants us. Dutiful kinsmen that we are, we will forgo our raid. I will ride back to camp with you, my lance untouched, my arrows unfletched, without a single camel, mare, stallion, goat, or chicken captured, since our uncle Saladeen wishes it so."

As the three of them rode back toward Essafeh's camp, Atiyah's spirits rose higher and higher. Adventure lay ahead, and sparring with Saladeen, and he would soon see Halima.

He heard the welcoming cries of the children, and from the corner of his eye, he saw Halima hurry with her mother to the tent opening, where poles swooped back the tent flaps to form a shady breeze-way. As soon as he found her, Atiyah looked straight ahead, his heart racing, his knees turned to water, pretending not to notice her presence.

Hassan and Ahmed delivered Atiyah directly to the greeting tent and stood bowing to Saladeen, grins of self-congratulation bobbing toward the carpet.

"Twice welcome and may Allah keep you, my nephew Atiyah! How grateful I am that you have called off your raid to honor your old kinsman!" Saladeen came toward Atiyah, his arms out-stretched.

Atiyah, suddenly wishing he were back in the desert alone, sank to his knees in front of his uncle and touched the man's soft hand to his forehead and to his chin.

Saladeen settled on a cushion. Atiyah squatted, balanced on bare feet, rocking slightly. Over coffee and pounded dates, Saladeen filled the air with compliments. Atiyah returned them truthlessly, heedless as a goatherd swatting flies.

"My excellent nephew, what will you do with your life?"

The question caught Atiyah off guard, and he froze.

"The future is one with the past and is in the hand of Allah," he answered cautiously.

"Each of us has a part in shaping the future," Saladeen pressed on. "The future is built of our efforts. What will your part be, Atiyah?"

To give himself time to think, Atiyah settled cross-legged on the carpet. "Uncle, I will accept any task that Allah puts before me. I will work hard to bring more glory and livestock to the Beni Khalid. I will strive to be brave and generous, and to walk in the footsteps of my uncle Essafeh."

"You would be a . . . desert sheikh, like Essafeh?"

He made a desert sheikh sound like a dung beetle. Atiyah could find no answer.

"Here in the desert," Saladeen continued, "the Beni Khalid are but one tribe, and a divided one at that, always in strife against others like ourselves. Perhaps, Atiyah, the task Allah has planned for you reaches beyond these . . . confines."

The dismissal in Saladeen's voice made Atiyah's head spin with anger and blurred his thoughts.

"Come with me!" Saladeen urged. "Come with me, and make your contribution be the glory of Islam and peace among the tribes."

Atiyah felt the hair rise on his scalp. Follow City

Saladeen to cursed Fez or Marrakesh? Send me to war, Uncle, as long as I don't have to ride beside a Shummari. But don't take me to the city!

Saladeen leaned forward, waiting for an answer.

"You are of the city, Uncle," Atiyah said carefully. "You know the ways of scholars and teachers. I am of the desert, and its ways are my ways. It is through the desert that the will of Allah is made known to me."

"Ah, Atiyah!" his uncle exclaimed, and smiled on him so dotingly that Atiyah squirmed. "You are truly a Gift of God, an angel among us. You are youth, and hope. You are a man of the desert, who wishes to follow in the footsteps of Essafeh, and yet you are wise. Your mind is supple and can grasp the wisdom of the *ulama,* the religious council, and make it understandable to Essafeh's people."

A terrible suspicion dawned on Atiyah.

"What is it that you wish me to do, Uncle Saladeen?"

Saladeen joined the tips of his fingers and leaned toward Atiyah, looking into his eyes and yet seeming to see beyond him. "I wish you to come with me to Fez, to meet his magnificence the caliph and to study at the Qaraouyine, the greatest university of Islam."

Study!

Read books?

Listen to clerics explain the world?

Sweat broke out on Atiyah's lip.

Saladeen continued: "I have no doubt that in time you will be chosen sheikh of the Beni Khalid. When that time comes, you must know the ways of the *ulama;* you must be equipped to lead all of our tribesmen, the city dwellers as well as those who still live under the black tents."

Atiyah clutched at a faint hope. "What if Essafeh requires me to stay in the desert with him?"

"Then, my nephew, the Beni Khalid will continue to pull against itself like a snake with two heads. Brother will lift hand against brother, tribe against tribe. . . ."

As Saladeen spoke on and on, Atiyah felt that he was already in some city, as if walls of unforgiving stone were closing tight around him.

"I will put the decision before my foster father," he said when he could stand no more of Saladeen's persuasions. He bowed out of the guest tent.

"May fleas devour you slowly," he said, once outside. "May Allah scatter scorpions in your path."

# 5

## A Riddle

**W**hich do you like better, Hassan or Ahmed?" Nazreen asked her sister as they slapped out flatbread for the griddle.

Halima shrugged. "They are exactly the same to me. Two grains of kasha."

"Well, they rode away before *you* even got up!"

"Were you peeking from under the tent, little lizard?"

Nazreen grinned.

"Tell me," Halima asked, "is our wide and wicked uncle gone, too?"

"Our wise and whiskered uncle is still here!" Nazreen raised her eyebrows and wiggled them at Halima.

"He doesn't seem to have heard that after three

days, a guest is as unwelcome as a spotted snake," Halima whispered.

"We'll find a way to tell him," Nazreen said.

Don't treat *me* as a guest," Saladeen implored that night. "Let me eat with the family. And with young Atiyah. It is rare that I have such a pleasure."

They ate outside, near the cook-fire, the women just after the men. When the food was finished, the bones buried, and the platters scoured with sand, Miriam began a game of riddles.

"Who can tell," she asked in her smoky voice, pausing to create suspense, "who can tell which of all things in the world is lightest, which is hottest, and which is sweetest?"

No one answered. In the gentle silence, each turned the possibilities in his mind. Finally Saladeen gave a long belch. "That is easy, O wife of my brother," he said. "The lightest thing in the world is a feather, the hottest is pepper, and the sweetest dates and honey!"

Nazreen giggled, and Halima tickled her to lend an excuse for her rudeness.

"*Ya Yimmah,* my mother, do I have permission to try an answer?" Halima asked.

"Please speak, my daughter," Miriam said, glad

to see Halima's spirits lifted. Halima gazed up at the sky above the fire, her ear bangles shining, her eyes half-closed. Even her brothers quieted to listen.

"*I* think, my mother, that the lightest thing in the world is a spark from our campfire, that nothing burns hotter than the heart of a person who is parted from her beloved, and that the sweetest thing on earth must be a bed full of happy daughters and sons."

"Disgusting!" said Nazreen, burying her face in her sister's lap.

A guffaw of pleasure burst from Essafeh. He waved both fists in the air, cheering. "Spoken like a true daughter of the desert!"

It was as close as he had come in these long three days to insulting his brother. Miriam grinned, a flash of strong teeth quickly hidden, and as quickly asked another riddle.

Halima turned her face to the stars, to keep herself from looking at Atiyah. Then she glanced at Saladeen. She wished suddenly that she hadn't made fun of him. In the moment that their eyes met, she felt marked: Saladeen would remember her, and always with dislike.

A breeze shifted the smoke of the fire toward Saladeen. He belched again, his eyes brimming with tears, and Halima turned quickly away.

# 6

## Uprooted

ight reached the world before color. Essafeh and Atiyah rode together over the dry hills, to count stock, to check on the grass, and to talk before Saladeen woke.

Atiyah was silent. What he had to say did not want to shape itself into words.

Essafeh discussed the livestock, each animal known and dear to them both. Atiyah made no response.

"What ails you, Nephew?" Essafeh asked at last. "Is it that you had no chance to raid our neighbors? You will again! Aren't you relieved that Saladeen won't be needing you for the caliph's army after all, as he has told me? Aren't you glad to be back among us?"

"Oh, Essafeh! There is nothing that would make me happier than to stay among you. Always!"

"And you will, of course. Where else would you be? So why such sadness, Nephew?" asked Essafeh gently. Tears had sprung to Atiyah's eyes and were streaming down his cheeks. Essafeh waited patiently until he regained control of his face and voice.

"My uncle Saladeen tells me that I lead a selfish life. He says that all my life, the world has danced before me as a bride dances before her bridegroom. He says that it is time I shoulder the burden of manhood and do those things I do not wish to do, for the sake of others."

"Atiyah!" Essafeh looked dismayed. "You've always done your share of the pasturing and the raiding, the hunting and tracking. . . . Of course the world dances before you, because you take joy in the world!" Essafeh's camel pranced with the enthusiasm of his words. Essafeh, wheeling, came close to Atiyah and looked him in the face. "Why do you look as if you are about to be swallowed by a ghoul, Nephew?"

Atiyah smiled in spite of himself. Essafeh's kind face was twisted with concern. Atiyah remembered the stories this uncle had once told him, of the monsters with teeth of silver and teeth of brass. He looked away.

"Saladeen wants me to go to Fez, to *study*," he said in a small voice.

Essafeh sat back on his camel, scowling.

"Is it possible, Atiyah, that Saladeen wants you at his side so that the caliph will think he leads all the Beni Khalid?"

"That may be," Atiyah said. "Saladeen says that if I don't go with him, those of the Beni Khalid who have followed him to Fez to fight in the jihad may turn against their brothers of the tribe. He says the Beni Khalid will fight among themselves like unruly dogs."

Essafeh pondered, even his camel keeping still for the moment. "Saladeen dishonors the Beni Khalid and all of the wisdom of the desert," he said at last. "What he loves and what he pretends to love are not the same."

"He pretends to love the tribe," said Atiyah.

"And he truly loves only to control. We are no more to him than chessmen." The words fell from Essafeh's mouth heavy as stones. He sighed, raised his eyebrows, and continued: "No Khalidi is like a dog, but the truth is that, by leading some to Fez in the name of the faith, my brother Saladeen has caused a rift between tribesmen. You could be useful in healing it, and you are *his* nephew, too. . . ."

"Then I should go, Essafeh?"

Essafeh looked out over the dry hills. "Saladeen will wish you to remain forever in Fez."

"He asks me to promise a year. More than that I would refuse. That much, twelve moons . . ." Atiyah's voice cracked.

Essafeh spoke quickly. "For twelve moons it will

[ 31 ]

be as an adventure. We will count the days with you, watching the waxing and waning of the same moon. . . ." Essafeh hesitated, then added, "Halima most of all will be waiting and counting."

The two men kicked their camels, clucking loudly, and raced homeward across the barren hills.

"You won't give her to Hassan?" Atiyah shouted, as if he didn't care.

"Oh! Ahmed is the more handsome, don't you think?" Essafeh shouted back.

"But she is promised to me, don't forget, Father," Atiyah called to the sky.

"Only to you! Only to you!" Essafeh whipped his camel to pass Atiyah.

Swear it in blood, Uncle, Atiyah begged silently. He knew no way to tell Essafeh that parting from Halima was a harsh hand that reached from nowhere and twisted him from his roots, sending him spinning, empty as tumbleweed.

"Who knows?" said Essafeh cheerfully, half to himself, as they slowed to a walk nearing the corral. "Perhaps if one of us learns the laws of the Prophet properly, Allah will reward us by sending us rain."

# 7

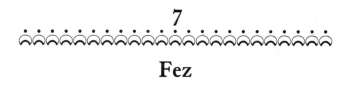

# Fez

Jn a high tower window of the library of Qaraouyine University, a sleepy student stretched discreetly and pinched his elbows to try to wake his brain. His dark, curly hair gave him an Arab look, but his light-skinned face and blue eyes marked him as a foreigner. Etienne looked out over the domes and minarets of Fez, out to the near hills, where gray storm clouds were gathering. The air had changed. It felt charged now, damp, and full of small expectant breezes. Down in the narrow streets, there was even more bustle than usual, merchants scrambling to gather in their wares, travelers dragging laden animals along toward shelter.

Etienne found it hard on ordinary afternoons to concentrate on the books he studied, even in the serenity and comfort of this great library. Today it was impossible.

Arabic! Why had he set his heart on learning Arabic? The ideas were elusive, and every word had many meanings. Etienne's careful European mind led him up one blind alley after another. Where he longed for definition, there was playfulness. What he pounded into his brain as fact was revealed a page later to be poetic fancy. The Arabic of the texts he studied was nothing like Fez street Arabic and not much like the everyday language of his fellow students. He went to bed at night with an aching head and a stiff neck from the strain of trying to follow conversations, and even in his dreams he struggled with a heavy tongue.

He ran his hand along the delicate twisted column that separated the window into two arches, framing the busy street scene below. Etienne wanted to walk and run and shout, to drop his polite foreigner's face, to sing loud, bawdy songs in French. He longed for his friends Thomas and Elenor, who would understand him, who would know when he meant to be funny and when he didn't.

Shrieks came from the street below, as children turned their dusty faces to the sky in anticipation of rain. One boy caught sight of Etienne and waved at him wildly. He and his companions began jumping and chanting together.

"Eh-tee-yen!"

"Eh-tee-yen!"

Etienne returned to the pulpit where he had been studying and gently closed the book he had been reading, centering it upon its pedestal, then covered it with an embroidered cloth. He went and thanked the Keeper of the Books with a deep bow, crept quietly down the tile stairs, hurried through the courtyard, and burst out into the Street of the Three Mules.

The street boys jumped onto him at the corner, clung to him tight as leeches, all shouting at once. He swung them in a dervish dance of knees and elbows, an explosion of pent-up energy.

"It's going to rain!" one told him.

"The flowers will bloom. Yellow flowers on the hills!"

"The horses will all have babies!" Is that what he said, Etienne wondered, or could it be a metaphor for something else?

"Go back to your mamas!" he told them, "because today I am climbing to the very top of the hills."

"We'll come."

The rising wind billowed people's robes and sent

dead palm branches rattling from the trees, swirling them down the streets.

"You can't," said Etienne, "because I'm going to run faster than the jackal."

*"Yaaaar!"* came a chorus of disgust. They had tried to keep up with him before on his mad runs, and failed.

"We'll come anyway," said one doubtfully, a scrawny, tough little boy called Jumei. Does his name really mean camel? thought Etienne. He has knees like a camel, but . . .

"Well," said Etienne, "I'll race you as far as the shop of Massoud."

And they were off, dodging people and mules, slipping on rotten fruit, jumping over fallen branches. Etienne slowed down just before he reached Massoud's shop, so that Jumei, in a burst of speed, overtook him.

"Jumei is the winner!" Etienne announced, locking his arms around the boy's thin heaving chest and holding him firmly at rest. "Greetings, Massoud. Allah grant you health!"

"Eh! It's young French, is it?" Massoud spoke from the darkness of his shop. Massoud, old and half-blind with cataracts, sold coffee to travelers just coming into the city. Unofficial keeper of the eastern gate of Fez, he stumbled out into the light of day to answer Etienne's greeting.

"What travelers have passed by today, Massoud?" Etienne asked, knowing that it would be the old man's pride to tell him.

"No one yet, young French, no one today."

Etienne smiled; people were streaming past, mostly leaving the city to return to their farms.

"But," said Massoud, grasping Etienne's arm and dropping his voice to a loud whisper, "I do hear tell there's a big sheikh from the court of the caliph who will pass through the gate this afternoon."

Jumei jumped with excitement, squirmed away from Etienne, and ran to tell the other boys. Out on the road, an officious man dressed in rags was shoving and shooing people with a palm branch. As the crowd fell back, a passage opened. Two tall camels, gently jangling bells and beads, padded regally through, ridden by two white-robed men of the desert.

They don't belong together, Etienne thought at once. One was young, with the pale frightened face of a boy and the dark eyebrows of a man. The other, Etienne recognized as Mullah Saladeen, a teacher at the University, though today he wore desert robes like the boy.

Massoud dug his fingers into Etienne's arm and croaked information to him, spraying him with saliva in his excitement: "That is the *wizir* Saladeen, adviser to the caliph, and the youngster is his nephew. It is said that the nephew is the finest young man of the powerful Beni Khalid, the desert tribesmen, and destined to lead them when he comes of age. He's been chosen to study the law, here at our Qaraouyine."

Etienne discreetly wiped his face on his sleeve as Massoud leaned toward him to whisper, "Let's hope he stables those camels outside the city. Those desert people! They don't even know that a camel stinks!" A toothless laugh welled up from Massoud's belly, and tears streamed from his squinted eyes.

Later, stopping to rest at the top of a hill overlooking Fez, Etienne wondered if the young man from the desert had already moved into the student sleeping-house and if he had been taunted because of his camel.

Etienne felt the first big drops of storm-rain falling on the hills, waking old smells in the ancient, complicated dirt.

# 8

## *Ins* or Djinn

A quick rainsquall pelted Qaraouyine University, washing away the dust. Then it moved off toward the sea, leaving the tiled minarets sparkling blue and gold, the flowers and leaves shining, the songbirds trilling in ecstasy.

Etienne, back from his run and already dry, slipped out of his sandals at the entrance and walked barefoot down the smooth red tiles past the concert hall and the library, past the banquet hall and the classrooms to the central courtyard where, every evening, the students gathered to talk before the call to prayer.

Today a buzz of excitement rose from the students who stood in groups under the arcade. Etienne looked for someone who might share news with him and noticed that many were glancing toward the garden in the middle of the atrium.

There, barefoot on the wet grass, his face turned to the sky, stood the boy from the desert. He was as still as a person whose soul is elsewhere. His eyes were closed.

During the evening prayers, Etienne saw the young man again, slight and alone. Crushed among the other students, the boy used a new prayer mat. He followed the rising and kneeling of the worshipers uncertainly, one step behind everyone else. In the middle of the prayers, a loud sneeze came from his corner. The prayer leader stopped. There was an accusing silence. Then prayers resumed.

Etienne wandered down the arcaded passages around the student gardens and finally found an old caretaker sweeping the tiles. He approached slowly, rehearsing a greeting.

"Blessings, Old Uncle," he said quietly. The sweeper didn't hear.

"Blessings," he tried, louder, touching the man's shoulder.

The caretaker jumped and dropped his broom. Etienne bent to pick it up for him. "Forgive me for surprising you, Uncle."

The caretaker's hands clutched the broom, frail as

bird's claws. "Ali Khaldun!" he corrected in a high whisper. "And had I known you were coming, young man, I would have spread mint and fragrant petals from your door to mine. . . . They call me Ali Khaldun, but shh! The prince is resting."

Etienne raised his eyebrows, and whispering now, like Ali Khaldun, he asked, "The boy from the desert, the new student, is he a prince?"

"A prince among princes," the old man answered, nodding. "He is asleep, though his dreams are troubled, may Allah guard him."

"Is he ill?" Etienne asked. Ali Khaldun leaned toward him, clutched his arm, and whispered, "Sick at heart, like a songbird in the hand. . . . A captive dreaming of escape."

Etienne took Ali Khaldun's head bobbing for a gesture of dismissal. "Good-night, Old Uncle," he said. "Rest well, Ali Khaldun." Then he thought that to Ali Khaldun, this standard greeting might sound too abrupt, so he added, "May your sleep bring you dreams of Paradise."

Was the boy really a prince? Etienne wondered. In Europe, princes were always surrounded by friends and relatives and hangers-on. But the boy from the desert was all alone.

In the night Etienne was wakened by a muffled cry that echoed in the arches, somewhere nearby.

Etienne dived into a robe and billowed like a ghost through the dark hallways, stumbling into Ali Khaldun. The caretaker squeaked with a sudden intake of breath and clasped Etienne's wrists with thin cool hands. Together they listened. They heard a loud sneeze, then a dignified sniffle.

Etienne spoke softly: "Is there someone who wants company tonight? Is anyone else awake, for I can't sleep."

In a moment, a light was struck, and two long brown hands appeared in the darkness, cupping the flame of the lamp until it steadied. Then the hands moved back, and Etienne saw the face of the boy from the desert, deep-shadowed and wary.

Ali Khaldun made a soothing sound, "Sho, sho, sho—," and moved back into the shadows, leaving Etienne standing alone.

"Welcome, fellow student," said the boy in classic Arabic. "Welcome, companion, and perhaps guide. Where in this labyrinth can one find the stars?"

Etienne paused, assembling in his mind polite

phrases of invitation. He found himself speaking like the texts he read: "Let us go to the roof of the library. Cool breezes play there, the rain is gone, and the moon will soon be rising."

"Let us go, then," said the boy, looking at Etienne oddly, averting his eyes when Etienne looked back at him. Etienne gathered up two of the flat pillows that were part of the student furnishings and set off through the halls and courts to the library. The boy from the desert followed like a shadow, and Ali Khaldun like the shadow of a shadow.

Etienne felt as if he were under an enchantment. He wanted to talk, but as the silence built, he found it harder and harder to break. At last they reached the rooftop. Ali Khaldun stayed in the stairway, moaning softly to himself and rubbing the joints of his hands. Etienne and the boy from the desert set their pillows on the roof and stretched out on their backs. The moon struggled up over one of the hills that surrounded the city, blotting out the stars with its brilliance. Etienne heard his companion give a deep sigh and turned to see him gazing at the moon, his wary look replaced by one of peace.

"I am called Atiyah," he said.

"The Gift of God."

"Yes."

Etienne glanced over to see if Atiyah looked embarrassed. He didn't.

"And I am called Etienne."

"Which means?"

"A saint who had rocks thrown at him."

Atiyah smiled a superior smile. "Are you *ins* or djinn?" he asked.

Etienne blinked. This boy must feel as he did that they were living inside a fairy tale.

"What exactly is the difference between *ins* and djinns?" he asked.

"*Ins* are made by Allah of potter's clay," Atiyah explained. "The djinn are made of smokeless fire."

Etienne picked up his own arm and let it flop by his side. Then he put his hand on his stomach, where he could feel his heart beating.

"I am both," he answered. "Potter's clay and fire." He smiled in the dark.

"*Ya!* You are *ins*!"

Etienne realized with a jolt that Atiyah didn't recognize him as human. Had he never seen a European person? "How do you know that I am *ins*, Atiyah?"

Atiyah laughed. "Because djinns are stupid. You are too smart to be a djinn."

"Djinns are not smart, eh? But they are powerful, I think."

Atiyah stretched and folded his hands behind his head. Etienne could see in the dark that he was smiling now.

"The djinn have the passion of the *ghibli* and a brain like a chickpea."

"I see," Etienne said. "And what is a *ghibli*?"

"A *ghibli*? You have never been caught in a *ghibli*? Where have you been since your birth? It is one of the great sandstorms, the one that blows from the south, across the sand sea. . . . Is there no *ghibli* in Fez?"

"I have been in Fez for three moons only. Fez is not my home. My home is in France, and in France there is no *ghibli*."

"France. Then you are Roum."

"I think so. Or some say French." Etienne had heard that the desert people called all Europeans Roum.

"And what brings you to Fez, Etienne-Roum?"

"I came to study. I studied Arabic in Toledo, in Spain, and then I came here to find people to talk to."

"Because you love to read signs?" Atiyah sounded disappointed.

Etienne didn't answer right away. Long ago, as a boy in France, he had decided to learn Arabic in order to convert Muslims to Christianity. Lately this ambition seemed absurd to him. By Atiyah's tone, Etienne guessed that he couldn't read.

"I do not love to read signs so much as I love to discover what they say," he said at last.

"*I* can read the signs in the desert; I can read patterns in the blown sand and the tracks of mice, even the signs in men's voices and in the clouds. The pictures written in the books mean nothing to me." Atiyah closed his eyes.

A look of sadness took over his face. "I have been here less than a full day, but already I am mocked. The youngest children know the Koran by memory. My mind fails to remember the words. Sometimes the words are not beautiful and must be rearranged. The teacher, this afternoon, was angry, and accused me of questioning the Prophet Muhammed himself. . . ."

Then he said, in a puzzled voice, "I should not be mocked. I am a son of the Beni Khalid." He gazed at the moon. His eyes were very bright with what might be tears.

"Tell me about the Beni Khalid," Etienne said.

Watching the sky softened to velvet by the moonlight, feeling the soft, damp wind, Atiyah talked of the desert, of Essafeh of spacious heart and open hand, of Miriam and Nazreen. Mostly and at length he talked of Halima, a girl who spoke poetry and chased frogs, a girl slim and strong as a date palm, fleet-footed as a gazelle.

Etienne listened and let the boy's word-pictures carry him into a world where poetry was as natural as air.

At last Etienne felt the loneliness he had come to associate with Fez floating away.

Stretched on the roof of the library, he took in every word, fighting off sleep, asking the few questions that would keep Atiyah talking.

# 9

## Moon Watching

Halima stood outside the sleeping tent, her hands on her hips, staring the moon straight in the face—the first full moon since Atiyah had gone. White and perfectly round, it tottered on the edge of an escarpment. "You may go on up in the sky and get small now," she said, encouraging it, releasing it.

Halima was proud of herself. She had worked hard and survived. She had herded goats with Nazreen, making up stories to pass the long days. She had lugged her sister Layla on her hip, since Miriam was advanced with child again and often tired. She had taken Miriam's place digging in the wadi bottom for roots that would hold moisture, and she had made three trips a day to the well instead of two, so that her mother could rest.

Eleven moons now until Atiyah's return. Tomorrow she would begin work on the next.

Y our turn, Halima," said Nazreen.

"But your stories are better," Halima said, too sleepy in the noon sun to spin a tale.

"You," said Nazreen, curling on her side in the dust, her head in Halima's lap. "I'm too hungry."

Halima sighed, then closed her eyes to get in the nighttime storytelling mood. "It happened, it did not happen, it could perhaps have happened in the tents of our neighbors, the Beni Salaan . . . ," she began. Nazreen snuggled contently into her lap.

"Mama Kanfushi and her adored daughter Amina were in the cooking part of the tent. Amina's father, Abu Jumei, was dozing in the quiet of the afternoon. Unexpected, unannounced, a guest arrived at their tent.

" 'Quick!' said Abu Jumei, shaking the tent flap. 'Quick, Kanfushi! We must prepare a feast for our guest!' Kanfushi sighed—yes, the way you just sighed, Nazreen. Do it again."

Nazreen sighed long and deep.

"But Kanfushi was a good wife, so she sent her adored daughter Amina to catch the last of the

[ 49 ]

chickens, two old chickens that were to be a feast for the little girl's birthday."

Another sigh rose from Nazreen. Halima rubbed her sister's shoulder and played with her hair.

"While the guest settled comfortably in the very spot where Abu Jumei had been napping, Kanfushi put the chickens in the pot, and ground her spices, and stewed the old chickens until the steam rose in fragrant billows and the tears ran down her little daughter's face. 'Here,' said Kanfushi to Amina. 'Let us see if the meat is tender.' She pulled a piece off and gave it to her child.

"Amina chewed and chewed. 'Well, Mother,' she decided, 'it is pretty good, but I'm not sure that it is quite ready yet. You try it.'

"Mama Kanfushi pinched off another morsel and popped it into her own mouth. She savored it slowly, swallowed, and frowned. 'It's getting close, but I think it could use a little more cooking. See what you think. . . .'

"So it went until there was nothing left of the birds but two necks. 'Please, Mother,' said Amina, 'may I eat these, too?'

"'Hush!' said the mother loudly. 'What shameful ways you have picked up from your father!' And she scooped some shriveled old dates onto a platter and carried them in to the waiting guest.

" 'That child!' she exclaimed, shaking her head as she set the dates before the guest. 'The habits she has!'

" 'What habit has her father taught your child?' asked the guest curiously.

"Kanfushi sighed. 'Whenever a guest arrives at our tent, my husband cuts off his ears and roasts them over the fire for his daughter to eat. It is a great shame how he spoils the girl.' She lifted the wall and slipped back into the cooking side of the tent. On the other side, the guest quietly gathered up his shoes and fled.

" 'What ails our guest? Why has he left in such a hurry?' asked Abu Jumei, rushing in from the goat pen, where he had been trying to eke out some milk for the feast.

" 'A fine guest *he* was!' Kanfushi exclaimed. 'He snatched both chickens out of my pot and ran away!'

"Abu Jumei hitched his robes up to his knees and gave chase, and as he ran, he shouted, 'Not both! Not both! Let me have one, at least!'

"His guest ran twice as fast and disappeared in a little puff of dust."

Nazreen, already half-asleep, smiled with her eyes shut, and pulled the edge of Halima's skirt over her face.

Will we move before the next moon?" Halima asked her father. They were sitting in the breezeway. Her mother grasped a lily root between her feet and pulled a heavy knife across it to scrape off the skin. Halima shredded the peeled roots for a stew. Miriam stopped her work and looked tiredly at Essafeh. Her face was thin now and her body huge.

"If we must move, we must." Essafeh chewed his thumb knuckle. "*Inshallah,* if God wills, we can stay here until the child is born." He picked up a root and took the knife from Miriam's hands. "Let me," he said, surprising Halima.

Halima was so bone-weary, she found she couldn't sleep. The darkness inside the tent was complete: To find out if her eyes were opened or closed, she had to touch them. She imagined herself a lump of date butter, melted in the sun, then poured onto the sand. She imagined herself flying through black night, turning restfully as an owl, the rush of warm air under her wings. . . .

The tent side—or was it the sky itself—dipped

once, twice. Rough felt brushed her cheek. She felt a moan through her dream that quivered the sand.

Halima sat up and shook sleepiness from her head, listening. She heard rapid breathing, short animal snufflings.

Halima lifted the tent side and stuck her head out into the night. She crawled out of the tent and found her mother doubled around one of the tent ropes, folded like a bat. Miriam's robe was bunched above her knees. Her long bare feet kicked and pounded the sand. Halima could hardly make out her mother's face in the darkness but saw that Miriam held the edge of her robe in her teeth, biting hard. The moans were coming from between her clenched teeth. Miriam noticed Halima, spit the robe from her mouth, and said, "Get a clean cloth." Then she clamped her jaws on her robe again.

Halima groped inside the sleeping tent, trying not to wake the younger children. Fear knotted her stomach and made her clumsy. She felt lonely for Miriam, as if her mother had gone to the far side of the moon and might never return.

From the clothes that had dried that day in the sun, Halima grabbed one of Essafeh's head covers and hurried to spread it between her mother's feet. The sand was wet there.

"Shall I call Father? Or our aunts?"

Miriam shook her head emphatically. Halima moved off, lonely and useless. Her mother had said to her once, "Giving birth is like death. It requires every bit of attention. You do it alone." But Halima wondered. Didn't giving birth involve other people? The father. The child. She tried to imagine Atiyah as a father and discovered that she didn't want to. What she wanted was to guess, with him, at what Miriam meant.

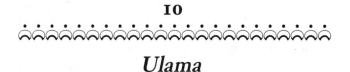

# 10

## *Ulama*

"Now I know what it is to be a falcon, hooded and jessed and at the beck and call of a master." Atiyah covered his eyes with his hands. He and Etienne were pacing around the court of the library between classes.

"If you are a trained falcon, who is your falcon master?" Etienne asked, pulling him aside so that he wouldn't collide with other students.

Atiyah snorted. "If only I knew!" He uncovered his eyes, stopped walking, and turned to Etienne. "The way in which I am like a falcon is this: I want to learn, the way a falcon wants to hunt. My mind is as ready to seek new knowledge as a free falcon is ready to circle and dive on prey.

"But someone else chooses what I should learn, even the times of day at which I should learn it. And someone else has purposes for my learning, and I am asked to learn without inquiring into those purposes, without questioning them—"

At the entrance to an inner court, a student was gesturing at Atiyah. Atiyah stared at him as if he had crawled from under a rock.

"They want you in class," Etienne explained.

Atiyah sagged. "Do you see, friend? And if I don't go in now, they will say that the Beni Khalid are discourteous."

"But this is the class taught by Mullah Saladeen, your uncle!"

Atiyah rolled his eyes.

"May I come in with you?" Etienne asked, wanting to know how uncle and nephew would talk to each other.

Atiyah put his hand on Etienne's shoulder, and together they passed through a horseshoe arch into the inner court, where students were already gathering at the feet of Saladeen.

And if the tribes did not fight among themselves—," Atiyah began.

"O respected Mullah," a student next to him prompted in a whisper, with a nudge.

"If the tribes, O respected Mullah, did not vie

with each other in cunning, in strength, and in generosity, then what would drive them to excel?"

Heads tilted, students glanced back at Atiyah, who had once again dared speak in class, dared question the lecturer.

Etienne held his breath.

"Wisdom, strength, and generosity are attributes of Allah," said Saladeen. "Attributes that believers strive to make their own through faith."

"Respected Mullah," Atiyah spoke up again, "would not a man be more likely to acquire these attributes living among those who know him? Why have you said that it is more virtuous for a believer to be one among many?"

"Because we humans are as the grains of sand in the desert, as the stars in the night sky. None of us, alone, is important."

"But the virtue of a leader is mirrored in the respect and well-being of his people."

"Islam is faith, Nephew, but the Prophet told us that it is also behavior. And Islamic behavior requires that the same harmony seen in a virtuous tribe also be expressed in humankind as a whole."

In the silence that followed, Etienne waited anxiously for other students to speak. The boy in front of Atiyah kissed the knuckle of his thumb and pressed it to his heart. All eyes were fixed on Saladeen, all minds drinking in his words.

Finally Etienne brought both hands together before his face to show that he wished to speak. "Respected Mullah," he said when he had been recognized, "might you tell us how the faith of Islam promotes harmony among men?"

"In terms that a Christian Roum could understand?" Saladeen asked, and several students laughed. Etienne reddened, but he managed to swallow his pride. "Please, respected Mullah."

"First," said Saladeen, "Islam recognizes one God so all-encompassing that human quarrels fade into insignificance.

"Second, prayers said daily at prescribed hours unite all believers as the spokes of a wheel, the center of which is the Holy City, while reminding them of their common purpose to praise Allah.

"Fasting reminds the faithful of the condition of most of mankind, which is want and hunger.

"The giving of alms reminds every believer that the good of the community is his responsibility.

"Pilgrimage brings together Arabs of every tribe and believers of every race."

In the silence that followed Saladeen's words, Etienne realized that he was leaning forward, his shoulders hunched, committing Saladeen's words to memory.

"Is the explanation pleasing to our guest, the Roum?"

"I thank you, respected Mullah. The explanation is pleasing."

Etienne sat in the courtyard, on a bench warmed by the sun. No one would bother him; the other students preferred shade and stayed under the arcades.

He was trying to remember and write down what Saladeen had said. He was shaken, chastened that a man he had dismissed as fatuous and false should turn out to have wisdom. There was something in the contradiction he needed to explore. . . .

He was aware of the swishing of Ali Khaldun's broom but kept writing, so accustomed had he grown to the old man's constant presence. Only when the broom sounds stopped and Etienne heard voices did he look up.

Saladeen was approaching, two young men crowding his elbow. He seemed irritated and was speaking harshly. "Hassan! Ahmed! What family I have!" Etienne heard him say. "What a hopeless generation! The two of you learn nothing because you are thick. Atiyah learns nothing because he is proud and intractable."

"Beg permission to speak, respected Mullah!" came the thin, high voice of Ali Khaldun. "The noble Atiyah is not unteachable! The noble Atiyah is distracted."

Saladeen turned to him with impatience. "And why would that be, Ali Khaldun?"

"Because he dreams, respected Mullah. He dreams of his cousin Halima."

Saladeen blew out his cheeks. "And I wish *that* one did not even exist!" he said, and swept away down the hall.

Etienne, who was still trying to be invisible, watched from the corner of his eye some horseplay between Hassan and Ahmed, who seemed suddenly cheered.

"Another ride to the sand sea will take us no more than a moon," he heard one say, but paid no mind.

# 11

# The Sand Sea

The thornbush and the desert grass had been burned by the sun and grazed away by the flocks. Far from Fez, the brown hills were bone-bare. Rain clouds rolled in from the west, but, like last year and the year before, none stopped over the sand sea where Essafeh camped. The Beni Khalid who followed Sheikh Essafeh were moving again; they hoped that in a few weeks the Wadi Hammamat would burst into bloom and they would find green grass, fresh thistles, and cyclamen.

Halima plunged gladly into the hard work of beating out the rugs and rolling them up, of scouring the copper trays and pans, of bundling up the family possessions, fitting one thing into another in intricate puzzles. Dreaming of Atiyah brought more loneliness than joy: She was afraid sometimes of remembering him more perfect than he was, undoing the reality of him. Hard work was better than dreaming. It filled her hours.

When each of the camels was loaded to capacity and each tied to the next, the chain they formed stretched into the distance like a river. Halima's arms ached from folding and lifting the heavy tents.

Halima's mother, Miriam, still weak and sad, had her own litter, a tiny house of blue cloth perched high on a camel's back, made comfortable with pillows. Layla and Aleya rode with Miriam, curled against her to comfort her for the loss of her infant son. Nazreen rode with an aunt. Halima had her own litter.

Halima's camel, Gamia, was the last of the caravan.

Men rode on horseback along the sides of the camel train, checking the loads. One stopped to tighten Gamia's girth: a clink of metal, a sharp jerk, a belch from Gamia. Halima reached out from the litter and scratched Gamia's neck. Then she turned to look one last time at their campsite.

The sands were already blowing softly over the dark places where their cook-fires and roasting pits had been. So much had happened there, to leave no trace. Atiyah was gone. Miriam's tiny stillborn baby was buried. The emptiness of the place where they had camped was both desolate and beautiful. Halima tried to shape her feeling of it into a tune, one Atiyah could play on his flute, so that he would feel it all as she did. . . .

The shouts of the camel drivers drove the beginnings of the tune into hiding, and Gamia lurched forward.

A sandstorm rose gently, the sand blowing soft and pink around the camels' legs. Halima welcomed the wind that flapped the curtains of her litter. Gamia's endless swaying, the swishing of sand, the soft warm wind lulled her, and she fell to dreaming, letting her thoughts float out to Atiyah, wherever he was. Her eyelids grew heavy, gritty, wearied by the glare. She tied the curtains close, curled up comfortably, and fell asleep.

In the gathering gloom, the sand swirled higher and higher. The wind howled and whined in Halima's dreams. She half woke, feeling anxious and groggy. When she lifted a curtain edge and peered outside, she saw figures huddled at Gamia's head. Their head cloths were pulled across their faces. She didn't recognize them; Essafeh must have sent them to calm and encourage her camel.

A few minutes later, while Halima slept, Gamia

tossed her head to dislodge sand from her eyelashes, and the rope that tied her to the caravan parted. She continued for a while to follow the others, then wandered aside.

Halima woke just before dawn, suddenly alert to the deep stillness around her. She stretched and tangled her feet in the curtains of the litter. She sat up in surprise and threw the curtains back.

As far as she could see, in every direction, were wavelets of sand. The sky arched overhead, a delicate pink.

Gamia had been sleeping, kneeling in the sand, and now the beast felt Halima stirring and raised her long neck. In the early light the camel was almost the same color as the sand, but warm, and furry and alive. Halima didn't dare leave her tiny blue tent, for fear Gamia would wander away and she would be totally alone.

Clutching the edges of her litter with both hands, Halima carefully slid her bare feet down Gamia's neck, stroking the thick fur with her toes, crooning gently.

Gamia was even-tempered as camels go; Essafeh had chosen his gentlest beast to carry his beloved daughter. But a camel's nature is to bite, and Halima carried scars.

She and Atiyah had pastured camels together, as children. They had sung to the camels, tedious singsong tunes. "It has to be boring," she remembered Atiyah whispering in her ear, his eyes shining bright close to hers, "because our brothers the camels are as dumb as gourds!" So they had made up words, a million words, and sung them to the same dumb tune, over and over.

This was the tune Halima sang now, to Gamia, lost in the desert. But the words she sang were whatever passed through her mind:

> "We're out in the pink sand, Gamia,
> And I don't know where we are.
> The night was long and my dreams were sweet,
> And we may have wandered far.
> But between my brains and your leathery feet
> We'll find the others soon—
> By day we'll follow the big red sun
> And by night the cold white moon."

The sun climbed ever higher, and Halima's head ached with the glare. The sky was very blue. Halima twice saw a hawk circle far overhead, and once she saw it dive. So there were small animals about, lizards at least, perhaps mice. That meant water somewhere, or wet roots. Her eyes scanned the far hills for traces of people, the near ones for plants that could lead her to moisture.

She found neither. Her eyelids and lower lip swelled in the sun. She lost all but the faintest croak of a voice. Gamia stopped listening to her songs.

She saw a boulder near the top of a ridge, thought for one soul-jolting moment that it might be a mounted person, and then, fending off despair, decided to shelter in its shade, where she would be noticeable should anyone be looking for her. She tore one of the litter curtains in strips, and with it she made a hobble and a lead for Gamia. She whispered to her as she tied on the hobble, trying to act calm, to convey calm to the animal.

> *"Gamia should have no fear,*
> *Gamia stay nice and near.*
> *Gamia has pretty toes*
> *And a stick right through her nose."*

The stick was for leading the camel, implanted when she was just born, but they had never needed to use it. Halima had nothing to tie the lead to.

Discouraged, she let it dangle. She spread another of the curtains in the shade of the rock; it was blue, the color of good fortune. She lay down to rest, trying to calm her body so that her strength would last. She tried not to think of Miriam, of how sad her mother would be to lose her eldest and her youngest in the same moon.

She thought of Saladeen, of the cold look in his eyes when Essafeh had approved her answer to Miriam's riddle.

She remembered the two men huddled at Gamia's head during the sandstorm. Had Gamia's lead been cut?

No, she thought. In the desert, no fellow humans were enemies.

The enemy was thirst.

# 12

# The Fountain

J n one of the inner courts of the Mosque and University of Qaraouyine, there was something so beautiful, so magical and strange that Atiyah thought when he first saw it that he must be dreaming. In the middle of the courtyard grew a flower of stone, open to the sky, and from its calyx spurted a stream of the most precious substance on earth: water. This was not the water dug so carefully from underground in the wadi, brown and heavy and life-giving. It was not like the yellow water the women carried on their heads from the well. Though it came through the stone flower, this was the kind of water that fell straight from the sky.

In the first days, Atiyah did not even dare to touch it, but every day he went to that courtyard and listened to the sound of the burbling flow, and finally one day he held out his hand like a cup and let the water fall into it. It was clear and almost invisible, a blessing of coolness.

In that same courtyard were stone benches, where students sometimes sat lost in thought or talking quietly. Fig trees and palm trees cast their shadows, dappling across the green grass, and birds darted from leaf to flower, calling each other into games.

When Atiyah and Etienne had first come there together, Etienne seemed neither surprised by the fountain nor reverent toward it.

To Atiyah this was outrageous.

"Etienne-Roum," Atiyah said, "look at this water."

Etienne looked.

"Listen to its voice."

Etienne obeyed, closing his eyes to hear better.

"Now," said Atiyah. He frowned severely at his friend. "Think of a sun so strong it sucks life away from every blade of grass."

Etienne nodded, his throat beginning to feel dry.

"Think of stalks so dry they break off and powder in your hand. There is no water. Animals are born, whimper, and die: Their mothers have no milk. Think of desert people, who pack and move time and time again, under the hot sun, following the herds. Men watch the skies for birds. Women and girls dig deep into the dry wadi to find damp roots to ease our thirst." Atiyah sighed.

Etienne opened his eyes and saw Atiyah hunched over in discouragement. Then his face lightened. "At last, one day, the gray and purple rain clouds roll in from the west and cover the face of the sun. They are beautiful. Women sing songs to them; my cousin and I plan to name our daughters for them.

"It used to be that every year one cloud at least would get away from the others, stand over our desert, and give down its clear, clean rain. Water such as you see there." Atiyah gestured toward the fountain.

"When this happens, know that the whole desert rejoices and bursts into bloom, Etienne-Roum! Grass grows up overnight, shouting greenness. Children run deep into the desert, picking flowers, wading in water, splashing up rainbows. The animals grow fat and glossy, the camels' humps are stiff again, and strong." Atiyah paused, his head back, his eyes closed. "This is why I am here, my brother."

Etienne, who had been lost in Atiyah's words, blinked.

"You are here, in Fez, because of the water?"

Atiyah looked at Etienne out of the corner of his eye. Would this Roum be able to understand? He rose and went to the fountain. He caught a little water in his hand and pressed it to his forehead and to his lips. Then he returned to sit beside Etienne.

"Listen, my brother. For more moons than we can count, it has not rained on the sand sea.

"I've been brought here to learn the Book, and the Sunna, the words of the law and the interpretations of the *qadis*. It is not because I love these books that I study them. How can I love them when my mind is full of my people and our herds, when Halima is there and I am here?"

"If you don't want to be a student, Atiyah, why do you stay at the University? Study is what people live for here."

"I hate to study, but I try to learn."

Again Atiyah gave Etienne a sidelong look and spoke carefully. "There is a saying among the peoples of the desert that it is the Archangel Gabriel who drives the rain clouds across the sky so fast and that he swings his goad with the sound of thunder, trying to keep the clouds from stopping over our desert. They say that this is because we, the Beni Khalid, do not strictly follow the teachings of the Prophet."

Atiyah closed his eyes, and just in that moment, he looked very old, startling Etienne. When he opened them, he continued: "We need more pasture for our flocks, if we are to stay on the sand sea. We need the clouds to stop and give us rain, so that the grass will grow, so that the goats and camels will fatten and multiply.

"For this I have tried to study, so that I might bring the law back to the Beni Khalid. I had hoped that in this way the Angel might drive more clouds to us."

Atiyah fell silent. Silently Etienne nodded, gazing at the fountain.

"And I thought you had come because Saladeen wanted you to strengthen his position with the caliph," Etienne said after a while. "I had it all figured out."

Atiyah smiled. "That is *his* reason, Saladeen's reason. But the clouds, they are my reason."

Behind them, old Ali Khaldun swept and swept the tiled patio, keeping it beautiful.

# 13

# Stick Doll

Halima was conscious only of her heartbeat against the sand. Its steady *swish-swish* spoke of life and liquid and gave her comfort.

High noon had passed. The shadow of the rock she lay beside lengthened. She could barely open her eyes, but when she did, it was no longer to piercing glare but to a swirl of colors: brown, tan, peach, and purple. A gap at the foot of the boulder framed a small stretch of desert, and she concentrated on watching this small patch, on stopping the swirling and making her eyes see clearly.

Suddenly her heart skipped a beat, and she dragged herself forward on her elbows.

Across that one tiny stretch rode a man on horseback, a falcon on his wrist.

Halima stumbled to her feet, and at the same time Gamia gave out a loud rumble, ending in a hiccup. The man reined in his horse and looked around. Unable to make a sound, Halima waved the curtain she had snatched up from the sand.

It was enough. Wiping his brow with his head cloth, the hunter made his way toward her.

Without a word he helped her into her litter and tied Gamia's lead to the horn of his horse's saddle.

A cluck deep in his throat set both animals moving. Then the man fell as silent as the tiny day-moon that glimmered in the afternoon sky. Halima herself could not force her questions from her swollen throat.

She had barely glimpsed the man's face. The falcon on his wrist, blind under its hood, turned its head, sensing her presence. Did its master have a face? Could he be a djinn?

Carefully Halima reached out her foot and touched the man's horse. Her toe hit solid flank. The horse, at least, was real.

At dusk Halima caught sight of dark rectangular tents grouped in the lee of a hill. Beside them were animal pens of packed earth roofed with old palm fronds. She heard the bleat of goats and the tinny sound of their bells.

Home! She slid off Gamia with a hoarse shout,

stumbling toward the tents, her arms reaching toward Miriam, Nazreen, Essafeh. The hunter, still mounted, stretched down to catch her shoulder, his grip an iron claw. Obediently she fell behind him. Her vision blurred.

These were not Essafeh's tents.

Her guide talked to a woman in the entrance of the *zenana,* their voices like bees droning.

"Mamoun," said a large woman with kohl-rimmed eyes, patting her own bosom. The woman's soft hands lifted Halima's traveling veil, touched Halima's face. In the rapidly murmured conversation, she heard the word *sheikh* repeated again and again. Who was the leader, the sheikh, of these people? An old man, probably. *Sheikh* meant old. Her father Essafeh was young for a sheikh.

She was ushered deep into the tents, past hanging walls that brushed the burned skin of her hands and arms like flails. Her sun-swollen eyes could see nothing, and she was grateful for the dark. Someone brought her cool yogurt and honey to drink, but quickly left, her thanks unanswered, her questions unasked.

"Rest," the voices said.

"Sleep."

"Quiet."

"Where did she come from?" she heard one voice ask another in the dark.

Then she was alone.

As her eyes grew accustomed to the gloom, she was able to make out shapes around her, and after a while a hand reached in and left a small oil lamp. Carpets covered the ground, feeling thick and new under her feet. Halima ran her hand over an embroidered pillow and held it close to her face, squinting to discern the pattern. It included some of the same shapes Miriam had taught her—"comb," "amulet," "tent of the pasha"—but on these pillows, the shapes were narrower, taller. Halima felt suddenly dizzy, as if she had seen a familiar face stretched and distorted.

She turned the pillow embroidery-side down and buried her face in her hands. Ouch! Her lip was sore and peeling, her eyelids big as fingers. Even her nose didn't seem to be her own. She was too tired and dry to cry, and besides, what was the use? She was alive. She longed for her own people, yes. But strangers would feed her, and she was in the shade. . . .

What would have happened if the silent hunter

had ridden another way? To stop her arms from shaking, she wrapped them around one of the strange, ugly pillows.

Footsteps again! The curtain dividing Halima's hideaway from the rest of the *zenana* was pulled aside, and someone peeped in at her. She turned quickly, but not quickly enough to see a face. She heard children giggling. I could grab one, she thought.

How must I look with my swollen eyes and ruined skin?

A few years ago, Atiyah had delighted in telling horror stories of people with the skin cooked from their faces, until one night Halima had dreamed of them and waked the whole camp screaming, and Miriam had banned stories altogether for a moon.

Suppose the children see me and run away and never come back?

The next time she heard the curtain pulled aside, she held stock-still. Something landed beside her with a thump: a rag tied around two sticks. The top stick had a doll face on it. Halima had not played stick dolls in a few years, but she picked up the bundle and cradled it. A giggle burst from beyond the curtain. Halima pretended not to notice. She rocked the doll and croaked a lullaby Miriam sang to her little sisters:

> *"Sleep, my child, my little camel,*
> *Sleep, my little treasure.*
> *We've rolled a rock over the lair of the djinn,*
> *And you are safe with Mother."*

Beyond the curtain, she heard children whispering. Aha! she thought. She sang another verse, making it up as she went along:

> *"Oh, my little daughter dear,*
> *Go and ask the moon,*
> *Go and find out who is here*
> *And if we'll meet them soon."*

Halima made the doll suddenly jump and go running about, looking under pillows and crying to itself, and finally she walked it over to the curtain. Not a sound came from the other side. How long can they hold their breath? she wondered.

Halima forced from her throat a tiny, shrill voice:

> *"Help us, Brothers! Help us, Sisters!*
> *Do not mind our ugly blisters.*
> *Come and tell us where we are.*
> *Come if you are near or far!"*

Silence. Scuffling of feet. Squeaks of argument.

Through the fold of the curtain near the floor came another doll, held by the small, grimy hand of someone invisible.

The doll danced around, saying nothing. Halima's doll followed it. More whisperings. The doll's voice cleared its throat and piped out:

> *"Stranger baby, stranger mother,*
> *Here am I, your little brother.*
> *Are you lost? Were you sent?*
> *This is a Shummari tent!"*

From behind the tent wall came a burst of laughter. Eyes shiny as wells in the oasis peeked around the edge of the curtain at Halima.

# 14

## Atiyah Sleeps

In Atiyah's dream a wind blew through an oasis, making the palm trees bend and shiver in darkness, tossing their branches over their heads in a wild and joyful dance. The whispers that flew from rustling tree to rippling branch were all poems. All the poetry of the desert swept into the oasis and tangled in the trees, to be spoken over and over and over by the wind.

Then, in his dream, Atiyah saw torches light the pathways between the trees, heard the voices of men. They came, small at first, but soon taller than the trees themselves. They threw restraining ropes around the tossing fronds, jerking them roughly into bundles. They pulled the bundles sideways, then hacked them from the wailing, struggling trunks.

The men disappeared from the oasis, dragging

behind them the poems, fettered in palm fronds. Atiyah the dreamer, nothing to him but hands grown huge and a longing to comfort, was left rubbing the poor shorn head of a tree. "Come back, song and birds and fruit. Come back, whispering poems." His tears ran through the rough-cut tree, watering it, killing it with salt.

Atiyah was crying and in pain, and with a sick feeling he woke to know that he was lying at the feet of the Keeper of the Books, in the library of the University, surrounded by books written on palm fronds, bound in bundles. The Keeper of the Books was hitting him with a staff.

"Disrespect," pronounced the caliph.

"Disrespect," echoed the two white-robed men who sat on either side of him. One of the two was the Keeper of the Books. The other was Saladeen.

Atiyah stood before them, on disciplinary probation for sleeping in the library.

"A lesser student would be expelled," said the caliph.

The two others nodded gravely. "Indeed," they murmured.

"But of this student, I require an explanation,"

said the caliph. "I would understand the thoughts of the future leader of the Beni Khalid."

Saladeen and the Keeper of the Books cleared their throats. Six brown eyes fastened on Atiyah's face.

"What would you like me to explain, O servant of the Prophet?" Atiyah asked politely.

"One hundred years ago," said the caliph, "it was decided that the city of Fez would host the foremost university in the world. Renowned scholars spent endless hours searching out and collecting the finest texts, the most beautiful verses, the most complete and detailed histories.

"The most accomplished and the most daring architects and builders were called upon, honored with the charge to design and construct the classrooms, the library, the courts, and walking places. Year after year they planned and labored, codified and collected.

"That the knowledge and wisdom of our forebears could be preserved and passed on to all generations, and the wisdom of each generation challenged and broadened and made useful—this was the purpose to which these great men dedicated their lives."

The caliph had leaned more and more toward

Atiyah as he spoke, and Atiyah braced to catch him should he topple from his throne. But the caliph had more on his mind, and as he barked out the next words, he sat straighter, distancing himself from Atiyah.

"*You,* Atiyah of the Beni Khalid, have shown disrespect for the labors of scholars and architects alike. Since your arrival in Fez, you have made yourself notable by questioning the texts of the Holy Book, by misreciting the poetry of great masters, and by sleeping among the most important books ever collected. What do you have to say for yourself?"

Atiyah stood very still, repeating in his mind the caliph's words. Was sleep an insult? Were dreams not to be valued? And how could he respond without questioning, and how could he question without showing further disrespect? The caliph's anger was like quicksand. Once in it, it was perhaps better not to move.

"Though in my ignorance I have not shown it correctly, I do deeply respect the work of those who built this university. Yes, also the work of those who write the books and of those who guard them." He bowed stiffly toward the Keeper of the Books. "As a son of the Beni Khalid, I would also say that knowledge and wisdom are far greater than can be contained in books or laws. The lion walks across the desert sand, leaving footprints behind him. By the next moon he is dead, his carcass devoured by vultures. His footprints blow away in the wind."

The caliph interrupted him. "And that is why, foolish boy, we need books and laws."

"The lion's beauty is such that it can't be collected or held. His beauty simply *is*."

"Is this an excuse for sleeping in the library?" The caliph's voice implied that he did not think so.

"The beauty that *is* can sometimes be apprehended through dreams," said Atiyah. This was the truest thing he could find in his heart to say, and as his eye fell on one of the caliph's red foot-pillows, more than anything he wanted to wrap his arms around it, stretch out on the white marble floor, and sleep.

# 15

# Wool Gathering

The Shummari camels were in molt. Their skin itched. They bellowed complaints, rubbed themselves against any stump or tall rock, left hair streaming from snags and twisted on thorns. Their coats fell in clumps to the ground.

Halima heard the camels' complaints from inside the Shummari guest tent, where she had been secluded for three long days. Only the bravest of the small children had thrown a few words her way, scampering off before she had time to reply.

Today the sun had not yet risen, and children were beating the tent side, yelling:

"Hair day!"

"It's hair day!"

"Everyone outside!"

"Mamoun says so!"

Halima jumped up and stuck her head out of the tent. The children were gone.

As she yawned and stretched, then dragged a robe over her head, Halima thought of how at home, all the women and girls would gather the camel hair, boil it, and beat it into felt, how they would choose teams and have a race to see which team could collect the most hair between sunup and sundown. At home, Nazreen would help her; they would gather hair and pile it in front of Miriam high as a mountain, and Atiyah, passing by, would raise his eyebrows and his thumbs and laugh, and they would win.

Here I will have to work alone, she thought, because nobody, *nobody*, will choose me. But if I stay inside another day, I will be like the sand-lion that digs his hole too deep and can never struggle free, and so dies trapped in his own hiding place. . . .

Outside the tents, women and girls gathered in the semidarkness, laughing and talking, glancing at Halima from the corners of their eyes. Halima longed for her mother. Was Miriam still sad? Of course! A sudden flight of swallows cut across the dawn sky, quick as a fist-throw of pebbles. If only she could send a swallow to tell her mother that she lived and loved her. Tears came to her eyes, and she hugged her empty basket tight against her chest.

Women were teaming up, calling for partners,

and Halima tried not to listen, to disappear into the half-light, not to care that no one even knew her name.

"I choose for my partner the stranger-guest!" called a young woman. Halima jumped like a djinn freed from a rock and ran with her heart in her throat to stand beside the one she'd heard the children call Saffiya.

The sky brightened to pink. A man staggered out of one of the tents, carrying in both arms a wide goatskin drum. As the women cheered and applauded, he settled down next to it, cross-legged, and waved a drumstick in the air. He fixed his eyes on the rim of hill where the sun would first appear. The women and girls turned with him and fell silent.

The sun edged up behind the farthest dune. Just as its first ray pierced Halima's eyes, the man beat a roll on the drum.

The women screamed and scattered, laughing, shouting taunts and challenges. Saffiya grabbed Halima by her sleeve and dragged her, breathless, over a ridge.

They scrambled, half-sliding, down a steep escarpment. They landed in a shower of shale in a crevasse where a row of tamarinds made shade cover for the stock. Saffiya, standing first, dusting off the back of her robe, grinned at Halima. "Today we must think like camels. You have heard them out here, scratching and keening? Unless you are deaf, you heard them, our wonderful singing camels. This is their favorite gathering spot. Are you ready, girl? To work, then!"

Saffiya and Halima filled a blanket with clumps from the ground, then set about pulling out the finer hair from the tamarinds.

Halima watched Saffiya's strong fingers, twisting and pulling as expertly as those of Miriam herself. She wanted to talk but was kept silent by shyness and by admiration for Saffiya, with her gold tooth and her golden eyes and her long braided red-black hair. And her fearlessness. It seemed that everyone in the camp had been told not to talk to Halima, and Saffiya had disobeyed.

"So, are you happy among us, Halima?" Saffiya asked in her Shummari accent.

"Oh, yes!" Halima exclaimed, and then, "Well, no!" She suddenly wanted to fling herself on the sand and scream and cry and complain. "Sometimes I want to bellow like a camel," she said instead, picking fiercely at the thorns, jerking out strands of hair, and stuffing them into her basket.

"Is that all?" Saffiya asked. "You have had an adventure, Halima, and I, for one, am hungry to hear of adventures."

Halima thought as she carefully separated wool from thorns.

"I grew up in the *zenana* of my mother, Miriam," she began slowly. "At night we heard the stories of ghouls with teeth of brass and teeth of silver, of djinns and princes and daughters of the pasha. In the day I worked as you work here, milking, herding. And my father taught me to ride, to herd camels."

"Did your father have many wives?" asked Saffiya.

"He has been sent courtesy wives, of course, because he is the sheikh. But my mother, Miriam—" Halima smiled suddenly—"my mother, Miriam, is his first wife."

Saffiya frowned. "Are there many children?" she asked.

"Miriam's children are six. And then—Atiyah."

"Atiyah is not your brother," Saffiya guessed, her eyebrows raised.

"Atiyah is my cousin. We have been betrothed from birth, in the way of my people. Is it done so among the Shummari?"

"Of course," said Saffiya, her voice growing hard. "How else would the clan stay pure and strong? I was betrothed to my cousin, my handsome older cousin. We were wed, amid dancing and praise-songs. We led the tribe together, he and I, and when it was time to seek new pastures, we rode together, our horses racing each other, and we sought out fertile places for our people and our herds."

Halima tried a question carefully.

"Does he . . . no longer live?"

Saffiya spat away hair that had floated into her mouth. "He lives, well enough. He chose other wives, wanting the children I could not bear for him."

"Doesn't he keep you, then, as his first wife?"

"If I so choose," said Saffiya with proud certainty, throwing back her long braid.

An explanation hung in the air. Halima waited, but Saffiya changed the subject.

"But you, poor girl, what will you do now? Where is your Atiyah, and why doesn't he come to rescue you?"

"He is gone, Saffiya. Gone into a life that I don't know and can't imagine. On a white camel he was taken to the city, to study the ways of the *ulama*."

"City ways," murmured Saffiya under her breath. "Quiet now, Halima—we have a visitor."

In a cloud of dust, a racing camel slowed to a walk on the far side of the tamarind. From where

Halima stood on the ground, the sheikh loomed so tall on his beast that he blocked out the sun. His face was too dark for her to see clearly, her eyes dazzled by the sunlight, which shot out in stabbing golden rays from behind his head cloth.

"Greetings, fair Saffiya!"

"Ill met, Cousin Raisulu. Why do you come to bother us?"

Halima, shocked by Saffiya's rudeness, dropped her eyes. So this must be the sheikh of the tribe, whose guest tent had given her shelter, must be Saffiya's cousin, and husband.

"I have come for an introduction, gracious Saffiya. Who is your young friend, whose face shines like moonlight on the homeward path? I have not had the joy of seeing her before."

Saffiya stayed absolutely still; yet it seemed to Halima that her body grew taller.

"This is Halima, a daughter of the Beni Khalid and a guest in our camp."

The word *guest* seemed to carry a warning and gave Halima hope that here, as among her people, a guest's honor and safety were to be preserved.

"Bring her to me tomorrow morning, Saffiya," the sheikh commanded.

Halima stood very straight, staring at the wool in her basket.

# 16

# Khaldun's Word

Etienne was trying to memorize a verse from the Koran. Pacing the red-tiled arcade that circled the patio of the fountain, he closed his eyes, the better to feel the sounds in his throat. Concentrating on the flow of words, he walked faster and faster, forgot to duck passing under an arch, and whacked his head so hard stars flared.

Reeling, trying not to shout in pain, he saw Ali Khaldun rushing toward him through a blur of tears.

"Eyes red with weeping and swollen like dumplings!" the old man wailed, and his high-pitched voice reverberated in Etienne's head.

"Cries like a she-camel that has lost its young, like a jackal in the full moon."

Etienne took hold of the man's frail shoulders

both to calm him and to keep from falling, but Ali Khaldun slipped through his hands like a sack of grain, fell to his knees, and grabbed Etienne around the ankles. Etienne swayed and sat down fast on the floor, just missing Ali Khaldun, the vaulted corridor spinning around him. Other students laughed in the distance. Etienne found Ali Khaldun's hand and patted it soothingly. "I'm all right, Old Uncle. I knocked my fool head on an arch, nothing worse."

"Not *you*!" Ali Khaldun broke in. *"Him!"*

Etienne sat back, disappointed. "Who, then?" he asked, rubbing his head.

"Word came to Mullah Saladeen, from his brother Sheikh Essafeh. And the mullah said to me, 'Go, Ali Khaldun. Go and tell Atiyah that his Halima is dead, lost on the great sand sea.'"

Etienne, already queasy, felt his skin go cold. "Ali Khaldun, speak slowly, please! You say that Halima, Atiyah's cousin Halima, is dead?"

"Lost and given up for dead on the great sand sea, the desert that has no mercy." Ali Khaldun broke into sobs.

"And you have told him?"

Ali Khaldun nodded.

"As if I myself had held a dagger to his breast and said, 'Die, my son.'"

"But you didn't. You didn't, Old Uncle! Where *is* Atiyah, Ali Khaldun?"

Etienne's mind was in a whirl. What would Atiyah do? Act first and think later.

Ali Khaldun gave a snort. "The prince has gone to Saladeen, to get horses. He will ride forth. He will not die until hope for his Halima is dead."

"Did he send you to me, Ali Khaldun?"

Ali Khaldun nodded, but Etienne didn't know if he had heard.

"I want to go with him, Uncle. I need your help. Will you help me find him?"

"He is at Mullah Saladeen's palace, in the new town, trying to get horses." Ali Khaldun's face twisted suddenly. His voice wavered and rose. "Saladeen will not give him horses. Saladeen cares nothing for Halima. Saladeen only wants to keep our prince captive in this town."

He began walking, hobbling rapidly, so that Etienne was hard put to keep up and to make out the old man's words.

"How do you know that Saladeen doesn't care about Halima? Isn't she his niece, the daughter of his brother?" he asked as they turned out into the street that led toward the new town.

"Saladeen has no heart. He promised to give me

[ 94 ]

gold, so I can buy medicine for my wife. He promised to give me work in my old age. 'Watch out for the boy,' he tells me, and 'How is the boy?' he asks me. But then he says, 'Be sure he stays here, Ali Khaldun, and if he should ever think of leaving, be sure you tell me before it is too late, or you will be the one to suffer.'" Ali Khaldun paused for breath, leaning against a wall. "Suffer," he muttered contemptuously. "There is no cauldron but has cooked a meal of mourning."

Etienne frowned, feeling his thoughts unravel and disperse. A meal of mourning? "Why do you think Saladeen will not give Atiyah horses?"

Ali Khaldun struggled to walk again and to talk at the same time. "Because—Ah! I have told you!—Saladeen wishes to keep our prince prisoner in Fez. The mullah will be glad Halima is dead. Our caliph himself wants Atiyah to become *ulama*. Bah! Even the rulers of our time do not fathom the heart of Atiyah."

They were crossing the bridge over into the new town, which was being built for the followers of the caliph. Newly planted gardens cascaded down to the river, already lush, and little windmills pumped water up to the top of the ridge to grow pomegranates for the wealthy.

Ali Khaldun pulled his burnoose closer around his face and staggered urgently toward a gate in a high wall. A guard greeted him by name, and they were given entrance.

Saladeen himself met them in the courtyard. Swishing his white robes across the blue tiles, he paced and turned, clasping their hands in his own, exhibiting grief and sympathy. Saladeen clapped his hands, and two servants came in, dragging Atiyah between them. They set him upright, unsteady as a rolled carpet. His face was hidden. His toes pointed strangely inward.

"Take my dear nephew," said Saladeen. "I give him into your care. See that he's kept safe. The poor boy has suffered a great shock. We've *all* suffered a shock! He must rest in bed until he has regained his strength and composure. Poor, poor boy!"

Etienne cleared his throat. "Might you lend us a horse, respected Mullah? Atiyah seems so weak...."

"The exercise will do him good," said Saladeen hastily.

Atiyah allowed himself to be handed over. Etienne guided him painstakingly out through the palace gates, and then slung him over one shoulder, locking his arms behind Atiyah's knees. Tiredly, he and Ali Khaldun retraced their steps down the steep streets to the river, then up again to the University on the other side.

At last they reached the door of Atiyah's student room.

Ali Khaldun sank onto a bench in the corridor, his hands pressed to his chest, breathing heavily. Etienne took Atiyah into his room and threw him down on the bed, then closed the door and leaned his head against it. He sighed wearily. His head ached. He considered whether to slap Atiyah's face with cold water and try to wake him or to take a nap first. A nap, he decided. A sound made him turn. Atiyah peeped out of his burnoose, his eye wary and lively as a bird's when it is hatching from the egg.

"Fooled *you*!" he said, raising an eyebrow, alert as ever.

Etienne collapsed on the window seat in relief. "Atiyah! You scoundrel. You made me carry you?! I thought you had been drugged!"

"So did the respected mullah. And I would have been, if I hadn't poured the coffee he gave me into one of his tiny-oases-in-a-jar."

Etienne opened his mouth, but Atiyah cut him short: "She is not dead, Etienne! If Halima were dead and gone from this world, there would be a blackness in my soul as deep as the space between the stars. Halima is alive somewhere. I'm off to find her."

Atiyah's eyes weren't swollen like dumplings; they flashed with enthusiasm. Etienne laughed, and laughing made his head throb. He reached up and felt a goose egg growing from his scalp.

"Horses," said Etienne. "Where can we get horses?"

Atiyah flung his arms around him with a shout. "You are coming, then! We will risk our lives. We will gallop across the sands, fleeter than moon shadows, never resting!"

"Where do we even begin to search, Atiyah?"

Atiyah slumped down suddenly on his cot, burying his head in his hands. Then he was up again, springing around the room.

"Here is what Saladeen heard from Essafeh: They were on their way from our summer camping place to the Wadi Hammamat. A sandstorm blew up. Her camel came untied from the others. Essafeh has searched all around their route. No traces."

"And the whole route lies through the desert?"

"Through a rocky part of the sand sea. Some Shummari have their tents pitched at some days' journey from the route Essafeh took, but they have seen no one."

Etienne, sitting on the other cot, opened his mouth again. He shut it slowly, thinking.

"Do you know these Shummari?"

"Ah! No. They are not good people. Not worth knowing. Maybe she tried to ride across the sand sea to Fez. Only for me would she leave her father."

"But Halima is wise, from what you say, and knows the desert. Surely she would have known that it is impossible to cross the sand sea alone, without provisions."

"Perhaps she had provisions."

"Atiyah!" Etienne broke in. "Listen! Ali Khaldun has told me Saladeen asked him to watch you here. Maybe he knows—"

Atiyah was on his feet. He threw open the door, calling for Ali Khaldun. Only a faint gurgle answered him. Ali Khaldun was slumped on the tiles of the corridor. Etienne and Atiyah lifted the old man gently and carried him to Atiyah's cot. There would be no use asking him questions. Ali Khaldun was dead.

# 17

# Gazelle

**H**alima was running alone in the desert. She passed a circle of rocks. In the bare space in the middle, a she-ghoul danced, her long breasts flapping like the empty sleeves on the clothes of women in mourning. Halima ran past, not wanting to see. The she-ghoul spun, lost in her dance of sorrow. Halima ran along the crumbling crest of a dune, just below the ridge. The soft sand slipped away under her feet. A hand reached toward her ankles. She struggled to run faster, but her feet dragged in the sand, too heavy to lift. The hand was gaining on her. Her legs grew heavier, pulling her ever deeper. . . .

She woke in a sweat, her hair sticking to her damp forehead. She was glad to be awake.

But she didn't want to think about visiting the sheikh.

The coffee grinders began their work, the beans rattling against the sides of the wooden mortars. Then the grinders picked up the rhythm of Raisulu's tribe: *ta-ta-TOOM, ta-ta-TOOM!*

Sitting on the carpet, staring bleakly at the dawn through the tent opening, Halima rested her forehead on her hands and tried to clear her mind of rebellion.

"Acceptance of sorrow makes the spirit strong," Miriam had told her a few long days ago. She remembered the tiny body of her new brother, so perfect, so beautiful, and so dead, and her mother's face as she had wrapped it carefully and handed it to Essafeh to bury.

Halima thought of days as beautiful as poems, full and joyful. Could missing Atiyah make her deep and true, as Miriam was deep and true? It didn't seem likely. She would never laugh again. Missing Atiyah was misery. Being with him was life itself.

As dawn lightened the gray-streaked sky, Halima saw a lone camel rider in the distance, and as he drew nearer, she recognized the sheikh Raisulu. He looked at the same time proud and insignificant, a doll-like figure suspended between sky and sand sea. She wondered if Saffiya was watching, if Saffiya still loved her cousin.

Saffiya stood in the breezeway, twisting the bracelets on her arm.

"Halima, our sheikh wishes to see you."

Raisulu was standing when Halima entered. The tent flap fell behind her. She stood motionless, waiting to see what his wishes would be. The sheikh loomed large and frightening now, too near in the enclosed space of the tent.

"Halima, Halima, this is your name?" Raisulu's voice was gruff. She heard without wishing to that he spoke to her not as to a foundling he would protect but as to a woman he wanted. She swallowed, fixed her eyes humbly on the carpet, and answered in words she had practiced over and over.

"Yes, Sheikh Raisulu. I am called Halima, daughter of Essafeh, of the Beni Khalid. I thank you and your people for saving me from the sand sea, for giving me shelter and food. I beg your protection for a time more, until your path shall meet that of my people or until one of my people comes to find me here."

"Aiee, Halima," the sheikh replied, and Halima looked up. "How far you wandered, on your brave camel! And how fortunate that my huntsman found you!

"I have traveled the sand sea all my life, and have I heard of the Beni Khalid? Have I heard of a man called—what was it?—Essafeh?"

The shock of his questions left Halima drained of hope. She had heard of the Shummari all her life, as villains in stories. The sand sea was vast, and its people insignificant in comparison. Yet weren't the Beni Khalid the greatest tribe in the desert?

She spoke to fill the emptiness: "My father has pledged me to my cousin Atiyah, also of the Beni Khalid. Atiyah has gone to study at the Qaraouyine, in the city of Fez. Maybe one day one of your people might travel to that city, and I could go and find him there." Her voice was brittle and her throat sore with holding back tears.

"Halima," he said once again, "the city of Fez is one I have heard of as one hears of a dream. If it exists at all, it is so far away that only the very hardy go there. The life you had, the plans your father made for you, they are finished."

He slapped the tent wall, and a powdering of sand sparkled for a moment, then was gone. Halima saw the shimmer and heard a roaring emptiness in her head.

But Sheikh Raisulu's voice kept on, saying her name more often than was needed. He interrupted her thoughts, compelling her attention with his staring gray eyes. A vein, a pulse, beat in his forehead, close to his eye. Halima's dream came back to her; she understood that the she-ghoul had been mourning barrenness.

"You have pledged your heart, Halima, but the one to whom you have pledged it is gone. There is no life that is not touched by sorrow. That you yourself are alive is due only to God's mercy. It is time now to accept the will of Allah, who has sent you to us."

Halima, empty of hope, heard the sheikh's words as if from very far away.

"Be my youngest wife, Halima. You will be esteemed above all others. You will be filled and bear fruit, and you will love our sons."

Halima held his gaze for a moment, then dropped her eyes. Like a frog in front of a rolling boulder, everything in her would be flattened by this man, by his sureness.

"But would it not be possible"—she faltered for a moment, thinking of Fez, thinking of Atiyah—"would it not be possible to seek my father, Essafeh?"

"I will not risk the sand sea for a foundling," said Raisulu at last. "But for my wife, I would do even that. I would risk my life to find Essafeh, the father of my wife."

As day followed day, Halima threw herself into the women's work as she had always done at home, helping Mamoun gather fuel, build fires, cook, boil and spread felt, and even, in her few leisure moments, working embroidery in the elongated forms of the Beni Shummar.

She had to make a decision, and in every task accomplished, every skill mastered, she was strengthening herself for that choice. Only a few moons ago, it had cost her nothing to be cheerful, to be helpful. Energy and patience had come naturally. Now every act was a conscious effort. It was as if she were sculpting a good woman out of stone, creating herself as she knew it was right that she should be. The enemy inside herself was anger: She had wandered into a trap whose dimensions she did not know, moved by forces outside her control. All she could do was make herself competent and useful. Then, Allah willing, wisdom would come.

She was not allowed to pasture the herds; Mamoun said she was too old. She volunteered to search for the thornbush and dried dung they used for fuel. This gave her a reason to walk well away from the camp, to see what lay beyond the stony ridges that surrounded them. But as often as she searched the far-off hills, she never saw a human, much less a rescuer from the Beni Khalid.

Alone on the hills, she talked to Atiyah as if he were there. "You told me the Shummari were *majnun,* demons, with glowing red eyes and horns and souls to match! And I believed you. . . . Is that a snake or a stick? . . . You'll just have to meet Saffiya. She tells me cousins are not so wonderful. She says I would do better to marry outside my own tribe anyway. Ah! Now you *will* think she's a demon."

Jt was Saffiya who reminded Halima of the time of exclusion.

Among the Shummari, as among her own people, it would be a discourtesy beyond imagining for a foundling such as herself to turn down the marriage proposal of a sheikh. A sheikh was allowed many wives, and many of those he took out of kindness.

But every day promised a chance, no matter how slim, of discovery by her people, and though Halima knew the sheikh assumed that she had accepted his proposal, she was not resigned to marry him. Saffiya comforted her with new knowledge: "Halima, you have three moons at least before he can wed you, so dry your tears."

"What gives me three moons, Saffiya?"

"Have you forgotten the time of exclusion? It is written in the Book that a man may not take a new-bought concubine or a foreign woman to wife until she has been in the care of his women for three full moons, that he may know that any child she bears will be his own and that she is not unclean."

Halima was both delighted and shocked. "Saffiya! Of course I'm not with child!" Then she remembered sneaking from the tent just a few moons ago, and her ears grew hot. "How could he think . . . It is not as if I were a bought concubine, having belonged to another, Saffiya!"

Saffiya put an arm around Halima's shoulders and shook her gently.

"*Ya Yimmah,* little sister, simmer down. I don't intend any slight on your honor. I remind you of the law, and I will remind both Mamoun and Raisulu himself of the law, just to gain you time."

Halima paced the tent, throwing pillows into a corner in a fit of agitation. She felt sick. Saffiya was trying to help. But Saffiya's words made the every-day, every-night misery of marriage to Raisulu all too imaginable.

A short while ago, she had willed the moon to speed its changes. Now she begged the moon to slow.

# 18

## *Moussem*

"Jumei!" Etienne exclaimed as they turned onto the Street of the Three Mules. "We need to buy a swift horse, maybe even two. Run and tell Uncle Massoud." Jumei was off.

"You have silver?" Atiyah asked as they hurried after him. Each carried a bundle of clothes and some flatbread from the university kitchen.

"I thought *you* would."

"Not one spot! My uncle Saladeen has supplied me but never with money. I would trade anything I own. But what? Bedcovers? A pillow for a horse? Pah! Here I am, the best horseman of the Beni Khalid, with nothing but a piece of city bread and a bag of rags."

Etienne was no better off than Atiyah. His knife, in its worn case, would bring very little. And how would he live without it? He had his sandals, his worn satchel, and a book of the sermons of Abelard, much discussed with Thomas on the long road through France.

Who could barter a book in Latin in a land of Arabs? If anyone could, it would be Massoud.

Before they reached Massoud's shop, Jumei ran back to them, bursting with excitement. "Etienne! Etienne-Roum! There is a *moussem*! With contests of running. Surely you can win! And there'll be riding contests for the prince!" He looked at Atiyah proudly as he said this. "The prince can ride better than anyone!"

"That's true," said Atiyah.

"Yes," said Massoud, a hand on the arm of each. "It is a *moussem,* only a day's walk away."

"Good," said Etienne.

"What is it?" asked Atiyah.

"The yearly gathering of all the finest horse traders, camel breeders, camel racers! Prayers! Feasts! How lucky you are to be young, and to have eyes!" said Massoud.

Evening came, and a wafer-thin moon struggled up into the sky. Footsore and hungry, Etienne and Atiyah climbed yet another of the rounded hills that seemed to roll forever to the east of Fez.

The Shummari have *always* been the enemies of the Beni Khalid," Atiyah stated, as if that explained everything.

"I know, I know," said Etienne. "They are bad people, and I wouldn't want to know them." He spit out a small tough olive he'd picked from a tree left to go wild in the barren landscape. "But just in case we meet any, since we are traveling toward their camp, I want you to tell me about them."

Atiyah looked up at the sky, where swallows were dipping and diving. "We should camp here," he suggested. "This is a land of plenty."

"If you will tell me about the Shummari."

Atiyah shook his head, chewing an olive.

"How can you eat those things?" Etienne wondered. "So, are the Shummari much like the Khalidi?"

Atiyah just stared at him, then looked away. "Like, and not like," he said thoughtfully. "Now that I have seen the ways of city people, I see that to them, we and the Beni Shummar would seem as like as these two olives." He opened his hand and popped the two last wizened olives into his mouth.

After much chewing, he added, "But to ourselves we are not."

"Tell me."

"Mmm. Like us, they are people of the hair tent, Beduin. They move from place to place. They pasture herds—goats and camels. They have some horses. Some of our horses, in fact, since they raid us whenever our backs are turned."

"And you, the Beni Khalid, raid them in turn?"

Atiyah's eyes sparkled. "Of course! *We* raid *them* even when they are watching! How do you think Essafeh's herds have become so numerous?"

"So the Beni Shummar are like the Beni Khalid, only the Beni Khalid think they're better than the Beni Shummar?"

"We *are* better," said Atiyah. "As the sun is better than the firefly. The Beni Khalid are better than *all* the tribes. The Beni Shummar are the worst."

"Absolutely," said Etienne. "Will we be well received in the camp of the Shummari?"

"Murderously," said Atiyah, his grin showing bits of black olive stuck in his teeth. "But first we have to find them. We have to ask any herdsmen that we see, ask at the water holes. . . . Are we near the sea?!"

Etienne was startled; if they were near the sea, they were even more lost than he'd thought. But there was a sound like surf.

· As they rounded the top of the hill, both saw a field of men, all facing east, bending together to touch their foreheads to the ground, then rising and voicing their praises in one roar. They ran to join them.

After prayers, each man rolled his prayer mat or spoke with his neighbor; people began to light campfires and go about the business of preparing the evening meal. Night was falling fast. Animals were outlined against the brightening fires; massive camels, donkeys still laden, horses prancing on thin, elegant legs. The night air was alive with whinnies and laughter, low argument, a tinkling of small brass bells, and the fluid run of a flute.

Atiyah and Etienne wandered among the campfires, lingering helplessly where smells of food were strongest. Traders curried their beasts in the firelight, drawing attention to their lustrous coats and healthy hooves. Young riders swaggered through, comparing mounts, laughing loudly over stories of last year's competitions.

"This *moussem* will be different," Atiyah informed Etienne.

"How do you know?" asked Etienne. "Have you ever been to a *moussem*?"

Atiyah shook his head. "Because *I*'m here!"

Etienne laughed. "The Gift of God has arrived!"

Atiyah, in spite of his hunger, clapped his hands above his head and danced in a circle.

Craftsmen and musicians congregated to take advantage of the crowds and the merriment. Etienne saw, in the light of the campfires, stacks of rounded earthenware pots, carpets and brass bangles, leather work of fine design, and rugs patched together from many-colored furs.

"Should we find someone to enter us in the races?" he asked anxiously.

Atiyah shrugged.

"Will you try horse racing or camel racing?"

Atiyah put a finger to his lips.

They followed running strands of music through the crowds until they came to a scene that brought them to a halt.

A laden camel, lying down, his hair glowing softly in the firelight against the dark blue sky, provided the setting for a group of three musicians: a flute player, who sat leaning back against the camel; a drummer, cross-legged, on his left; and a boy playing a rebec on his right, his foot up on a rock. All three had their eyes shut and swayed gently to the rhythm of the music, conjuring it slowly out of some shared dream.

At a little distance, another man stopped, put down a pack, and sat leaning against it. "That man," Atiyah whispered, "has been on many raids. He is like Essafeh. . . . " He glanced at the darkness behind the camel, and a look of loneliness crossed his face.

A small crowd was gathering.

When the man who had been leaning on the pack spoke, Etienne thought at first that it was simply to call for a drink of tea. There was a shift in the crowd. As the musicians moved into an accompaniment, Etienne realized that the man was improvising poetry, and he leaned forward to catch the words:

*"In the dark of the night, I rode alone across the desert,*
*And I heard in the wind a howl as from another world,*
*A howl of pain that could have been the voice of my*
*        own sorrow,*
*Of the loneliness that welled up in my soul.*
*I spurred my horse, my aged cob, toward the sound*
*And found a djinn, crushed under the weight of a great*
*        rock.*
*Sliding from my horse, I threw my weight against the*
*        rock,*
*And slowly it moved. The horrible djinn sat up*
*And looked at me with reddened eyes.*
*'Kill me,' I said. 'You will do me joy.*
*Free me from this life, which no longer holds anything*
*        for me.'*
*And the djinn looked at me, looked through me,*
*And ages later spoke:*
*'I will reward you, puny man, but not with death.*
*You are not yet ready to talk to the Angels.*
*Three wishes make, three wishes to restore your life.'*

*"So I thought and I thought, How to begin again?*
*And I said, 'Friend djinn,*
*Give me a woman with a face like the moon, who stands in a*
*Large and shade-giving tent.*
*Give me a red mare who runs fast under the hot sun, and*
*A loyal band of brave men at my side.*
*Give me goats and sheep, and camels with udders full of milk,*
*Much meat for my guests to eat their fill.' "*

There were rumbles of approval from the crowd, and Etienne caught the word *Amin* several times, spoken in assent. Men crowded around the poet, and he was escorted away to a campfire. To be fed, Etienne thought enviously.

But the musicians and much of the crowd stayed, and with them Atiyah and Etienne. There was a time of expectancy, the music low and tentative. Etienne saw eyes roving round the crowd, looking for another who would speak. Then, without even standing, one of the camel drivers threw back his head, straightened his back, and, eyes closed, commanded the attention of the crowd. He was dressed in rags; the polished knobs of his shoulders shone through the holes in his shirt. He wore no head cloth, but only a rag twisted into his dusty curly hair.

His face bore the scars of many fights. With eyes still shut, he began to hum, the sound high—penetrating and nasal. His face looked brutish at first, and annoyed, as if his own humming were a pesky fly buzzing around his head. Etienne watched in fascination. Slowly, as he hummed, the camel driver's face relaxed. He began to sing:

> *"There are people,*
> *People in the city of Fez,*
> *Who call themselves people,*
> *Even though they are more like*
> *Pigs. Hmmm."*

The crowd gave a little gasp, and some people spat, and Etienne realized he had never heard pigs even mentioned in the Maghreb, so unclean were they considered in Islam that the very word seemed dirty. But the camel driver continued unperturbed:

> *"These people say to themselves*
> *And to each other murmur that,*
> *If they wish to live in ease,*
> *They must not give alms,*
> *They must not feast their guests.*
> *Pah!*
> *There is no joy in their ease.*
> *Only the generous can have joy.*

*They would rather be fat than generous.*
*May they never drink clear water!"*

There was a shout at the end of his song. Someone threw him a coin, and a woman brought him a loaf of flatbread. He grinned and picked his teeth, all the anger gone from his face.

The musicians played wildly for a while and then settled back to what Etienne was coming to recognize as their waiting music.

Then, to Etienne's surprise, Atiyah stood forth. Slim and strong, princely even in his travel-stained robe, he bowed his head a moment, as if asking the indulgence of the crowd. Then he stood in the silence, looking into the fire, and when he spoke, it was in a gentle voice, the voice in which he had first told Etienne about his people.

*"Far to the west the thunderheads gather,*
*Ample mothers grumbling among themselves.*
*Lightning stabs the desert with its adder tongue.*
*Feeling the sudden coolness,*
*The gazelle trembles and*
*Cannot decide which way to run.*
*My cousin, my love,*
*Glances at the sky,*
*And like the kaikal bird*
*Pushing its young to safety,*

[ 117 ]

*She gathers the herds and runs among them*
*With comforting cries,*
*Until they are safely sheltered."*

No one responded for a few moments after Atiyah spoke, and then there was a soft groan from the crowd, a sound that spread like a contented sigh. Atiyah squatted and rocked back on his heels. A man from the crowd came over and touched him on the shoulder, beckoning him to follow. Atiyah and Etienne followed the man beyond the edge of the crowd, to the shadows behind the camel.

"Ask if you can race tomorrow," Etienne whispered to Atiyah. "Ask for food."

The man turned. "Your words have touched me. What may I give you in thanks?"

As if he had expected this question, Atiyah answered, "Lend us two horses, Brother, and they will be returned to you tenfold, at the time of the next *moussem*!"

"Why wait?" he asked Etienne, tossing his head sideways.

That night, Etienne and Atiyah ate hot stew, and early the next morning, just as the competitors were gathering to begin the races, they rode away on fine young horses.

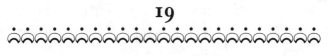

# 19

# Bride-Price

**H**alima sat on a ridge overlooking the Shummari camp, the brush she had been gathering all afternoon piled by her side. Mamoun knew now that she would not try to run away and allowed her to forage far and wide.

Smells of cooking rose with the spirals of smoke into the evening sky. Halima breathed the cool, clear air and listened to the squeals of children from the camp.

As far as she could see, dunes and hillocks caught the last light and glowed with the warmth and softness of apricots, while shadows deepened on the surfaces that faced the night. Patches of brown offered quiet promise of sustenance for goats and camels, enough for a moon or more. The black tents absorbed light. Their pleasing shapes, rectangular yet with gently curved lines, were so dark that they seemed to Halima as peaceful as sleep itself. The air above the roasting pit shimmered and changed shape like the djinn who rose from a lamp in the stories. I beg a wish, please, admirable djinn, thought Halima. Give me Atiyah to watch this evening with me.

She buried her smile against her knees. She should go help with dinner. It was the first time in many days that she had been hungry. She could see the other women and girls down near the roasting pits, taking turns stirring the cauldron of kasha that Mamoun had set over the fire.

Halima took one long look around her, reluctant to leave the ridge. A cloud of dust on the side away from the camp, where the camels were being herded toward an enclosure, drew her attention. Two men rode among the herd: One was the brander; the other was the sheikh.

Still as a stone, her happiness gone, Halima watched.

Raisulu rode among his camels, pointing out one and then another. Necklaces of blue braid were looped over the herdsman's saddle pommel. As he rode up beside each beast the sheikh chose, he slipped a blue circlet around its neck.

The sheikh was assembling her bride-price.

"This one!" Raisulu shouted, his voice carrying thinly from below. "And that one . . . a beauty!"

One by one, he pointed out his best camels.

"Take this one, too," he called to the herdsman. "She's the best. She always drops twins."

What a sham it was, Halima thought, grinding her teeth. Sheikh Raisulu was choosing his best animals, which would be given to her and then, because her father was lost to her, would go to rejoin the sheikh's own herd.

She had so little time left. Two more moons had come and gone.

Slowly she stood and gathered up the pile of brush, hugging it against her chest, thorns and all, not minding the pain. She felt her way down from the ridge, her toes digging deep into the cooling sand.

Halima! Come quickly!" Saffiya flew like a dust devil around the side of the tent to where Halima was scouring the kasha pot. Her face was flushed, her eyes flashing. She dropped to her hands and knees beside Halima and whispered urgently, "Two strangers have arrived at the guest tent. One is asking for hospitality in an accent like yours, and one is a foreigner, a Roum, with eyes like sky!"

Halima threw her scraper in the air and jumped to her feet. She grabbed Saffiya, hugged her, and stood back, biting her lip. "What—" She searched Saffiya's face, waiting for a plan to take shape between her sparkling eyes.

Together they ran to the cooking tent. From there, standing on tiptoe, they could peek through a parted seam into the guest tent.

"Is it him? Is it your Atiyah?"

For a moment all Halima could see was Mamoun's back, as she spoke words of guarded greeting. Move, Mamoun! thought Halima so hard she felt she could shift mountains. Mamoun stepped aside, and Halima found herself looking straight at Atiyah.

He was so close that her heart leaped to her throat and pushed out a squeak. She clapped both hands over her mouth, looking wide-eyed at Saffiya.

Saffiya didn't need to ask who the stranger was. "They are in danger, Halima," she whispered. "If Raisulu knows they're here, he'll kill them."

"Why?" asked Halima. "Doesn't Raisulu follow the code of the desert, the guest friendship?"

"Of course he must," said Saffiya with more confidence than she felt. "Quick, Halima, we must feed the guests to assure their guest status. Once they've eaten under his roof, even Raisulu can't harm them. But Sister"—she hesitated with a hand on Halima's

[ 122 ]

arm—"Raisulu will be jealous of Atiyah. Understand, Halima, that he will wish your Atiyah ill."

Halima hugged herself and shivered. Then she spun around and poked up the cook-fire. "Hurry, then, Saffiya! Get the flour!"

When Mamoun came in to tell them to prepare food for guests, Saffiya was already heating the griddle over the embers and Halima was kneading the dough. No sooner had she divided the dough and slapped it into rounds than the baking tray was hot and ready to receive it. Halima threw disk after disk onto the hot metal, while Saffiya lifted the baked rounds and spread them with date butter.

Halima carried the tray in to serve Atiyah, her hands trembling. Saffiya came behind her, carrying the tea urn, and bumped into Halima's back. Atiyah and Halima were staring at each other.

"Welcome, Cousin, and well met," Halima managed to say at last. "This hour is a blessing from the Compassionate."

They set down the food, and Saffiya bade the guests eat. Then she put her hand on Halima's arm and dragged her to the cooking side of the tent.

Halima burst into sobs, rocked in Saffiya's arms. "I want to go back! Saffiya! Why couldn't I think what to say? I *never* find the right words!"

Saffiya patted her gently on the back and held her

steadily until her shaking subsided. "The Gift of God was speechless, too," she commented at last, and Halima laughed.

"He must not have been Atiyah after all," she said, wiping her eyes with the back of her hand.

Saffiya lifted the tent side and looked out into the dusk.

"Raisulu is back."

Through the tent seam, Halima and Saffiya watched Raisulu enter the guest tent. They saw Atiyah and Etienne rise and bow.

"Travelers!" came Raisulu's growl. The word hung in the air. Then: "I see that you are partaking of guest friendship. In the name of Allah the All-Merciful, you are welcome. But may I ask whom I have the honor of feeding in my tent?"

Atiyah stood straight and pale.

"This is Etienne-Roum, a student from across the sea, and I am Atiyah, of the Beni Khalid." Atiyah bowed politely, his hands on his knees. Etienne quickly imitated him.

Raisulu rumbled something, but because he had his back to her, Halima could not hear his words.

Atiyah spoke again: "I know that our people have been enemies in the past. I do not come to you as to an enemy. I am grateful for your generous hospitality and still more grateful for your help in searching for, finding, and sheltering my cousin Halima." He paused.

There was no response from Sheikh Raisulu.

"We see, by the fact that she is well within your tents, that your people have been gentle in restoring her to health. We have confidence in your kindness in planning to return her to her father, Essafeh."

Halima held her breath. Atiyah had spoken respectfully to a Shummari! She wished she could see Raisulu's face.

Atiyah had outlined for the sheikh the only course of action he could honorably take. Halima clenched her hands, willing Raisulu to understand.

She saw Raisulu nod and was swept with happiness.

But Sheikh Raisulu surprised her. "Halima is indeed here," he said calmly. "She has honored us by agreeing to be my wife."

Atiyah stepped back as if he'd been stung.

Saffiya squeezed Halima's arm, then slid quickly into the guest tent and bowed before the sheikh.

"Since it is our custom to discuss weighty matters only when our guests are well rested, should I take them to their sleeping tent, Master?"

There was silence in the tent, fragile and tense.

"Do that, Saffiya," Raisulu conceded at last.

# 20

# Three Tents

Etienne didn't dare look at Atiyah. He followed the woman who was leading them to the guest tent, allowing himself to be mesmerized by the thick braid of reddish black hair that swung down her back.

She was robed in black from head to toe, so mysterious to him that he had to remind himself that, just like him, she had a complicated everyday life of her own. He had watched her face in the guest tent to avoid gawking at Halima, of whom he had heard so much. Her face had reflected anxiety, compassion, and maybe humor. The sheikh had called her Saffiya. Was this Arabic for Sophia? Did her name mean Wisdom?

With sincerity and faulty grammar, he murmured his thanks to her as she left them, adding, "Tell Halima of our joy in finding her alive."

For the first time he saw Saffiya smile, revealing a gold tooth. Bowing her head, she glided out of the tent.

Atiyah, berserk, paid no attention to Saffiya.

He paced the small sleeping tent, punching its wall with his fist, making the dust fly.

"*Ya Yimmah!* Etienne-Roum, what do we do now? Halima is alive, Allah be praised, but oh! I want to howl like the coyote, shriek like the hyena. Marry Raisulu? How could she? A Shummari?! He seems a man of faith. . . . If she had told him she was pledged to me, would he claim her? And if she has not told him, why not? Could she prefer him to me? That gray-eyed ghoul? Impossible!"

Etienne let Atiyah rave on. Nonsense was preferable to mute misery, and he needed time to think. Etienne wondered if in fact Raisulu was a man of faith, for if he was, why hadn't he restored Halima to her father long since?

"If I could be sure that Halima was still Halima," Atiyah was saying, "I would claim her as my cousin, my betrothed. Then a *good* sheikh, even a Shummari, would send her home with gifts and blessings. But if Raisulu is a regular Shummari, he will kill me—and you—and keep Halima for himself, the fiend, telling no one. And if we were to escape tonight and tell Essafeh, there would be war between the tribes. Raisulu would take his vengeance by killing Halima."

"Much rests on his being a man of faith," said Etienne.

"Eeh!" exclaimed Atiyah impatiently. "Why do we discuss the faith of Raisulu? It's the faith of Halima that concerns me, for if she prefers that old sheikh to me, then I don't care a fig if I live or die, and the more wars among the tribes, the better!"

Etienne jumped to his feet. "*Enough!* Just listen for once, Atiyah!"

The anger in his voice surprised him and caught Atiyah's attention.

"Halima has not made this choice freely. I saw her face when she saw you. It was the face of one who looks on her beloved, whom she did not expect to see again."

"For all you know!" said Atiyah, but he looked relieved.

In the women's tent, Halima bit her fingernails and stomped around the small space like a caged mountain lion.

"I'll go to Raisulu, Saffiya. I let him believe I would marry him. I should have said no a thousand times! I didn't dare to hope that I would see Atiyah again. Surely the sheikh won't make me marry him now that Atiyah is here."

"He may, Halima," said Saffiya quietly. "Here, among the Beni Shummar, Raisulu is more powerful than Atiyah. Raisulu is a man who will stop at nothing to get what he wants. For days he has been collecting your bride-price."

"Saffiya?"

Saffiya turned toward her slowly.

"You love Raisulu?"

Saffiya nodded grimly.

"Raisulu is a good man, strong and intelligent. . . ." It was almost a question.

"Strong and intelligent, yes," Saffiya answered. "But not always good. He can be cruel, and greedy. . . ."

"He knows of the Beni Khalid. . . ."

"He knows them well."

"He misled me on purpose."

"And he will say that *you* misled *him*."

"Was it you who left him, then?"

Saffiya smiled sadly. "If you call this leaving him. I suffer beside him, uselessly.

"For years, I thought we were of one mind. Then I saw him slip into shoddy ways, caring more for himself than for his people. And I argued with him.

[ 129 ]

I drove him further away. Better, I decided, to do what I myself could do well alone than to add my strength to his for purposes to which I could not agree."

Halima looked at her friend, recognizing her power, her steadfastness. "Life isn't over," she said.

"Do we dare hope?" Saffiya asked, with a glimmer of her old spark.

Grudgingly Raisulu allowed Halima into his presence. He rose as she came in, but turned sideways to her and said nothing.

"I have come to beg a boon of you, knowing you to be a fair and generous man," said Halima.

Raisulu nodded curtly. At least she would be allowed to speak.

"I was honored when you asked me to be your wife." Halima took a deep breath. She cleared her mind and her throat of anger. "You are the sheikh, chosen by your people because of your merits, because of those qualities that have importance among our people—bravery in battle, wisdom in settling the matters of the people, adherence to the traditions of the Beni Shummar.

"The Shummari chose you because they knew you were a man of honor in whom they could put

[ 130 ]

their trust. As my father, Essafeh, was chosen by the Beni Khalid, you were chosen by the Beni Shummar.

"You and I are of two great tribes, which follow the same wisdom."

Halima paused, struggling to unwind in her mind the complicated skeins of thought. Raisulu watched her, saying nothing.

"I was raised to be the wife of a sheikh, to help lead a great tribe. As your wife, I hoped to be the person I was raised to be. A person of whom my father would be proud."

She looked up at him, meeting his eyes. Raisulu nodded.

"And we could have brought each other joy."

Raisulu turned away. Halima spoke again.

"But our laws go deeper. The traditions of both our tribes speak differently now. Atiyah and I were betrothed at birth. His claim on me is stronger than yours. For the sake of your honor among the tribes, I beg you to release me to him."

Raisulu spoke at last, his voice heavy, as if he dragged his words from far away.

"Tomorrow the wedding celebration will be held. Your cousin and the foreigner may come, as guests."

He turned, lifted the flap, and left the tent.

# 21

# The Fool

Halima lay on her pallet, staring into the darkness. The weary hours of the night crept by. What had she said wrong? "We could have brought each other joy." What a lie. She had said it to please, to soften her thoughts, not because she meant it. Forms of politeness, half-truths were making her blind; her confusion brought memories of groping along in a sandstorm once when she was very young, blinded and completely disoriented.

Then she had had a hand to hang on to: Essafeh's. "There's not much you can be sure of in a sandstorm," he had said. "If you glimpse stars or the moon, that way is up. If the sand begins to cover you, reach your hand toward the sky. After a storm, when the dunes have changed shape and the shrubs you used to guide you are covered, look at the stars.

Find the truth star, the one we count on not to change."

Remembering Essafeh's words calmed Halima. She lifted the tent flap and let the cool air blow on her sweaty face. She looked at all the familiar constellations, and finally her eyes rested on the truth star. It looked small and cold.

"What is my truth?" she asked herself aloud. "What do I really know?"

She remembered a hot day with Atiyah when they were both children. Atiyah was jabbing at ants with his forefinger, killing them. She was furious with him, so mad she had a big lump in her throat. She remembered a fight they'd had while pasturing camels—both leaning against the same tree, their backs to each other, in a huff until both turned at the same time and caught each other's eye. She remembered Atiyah bleeding from the head, kicked by his own horse because he was trying to slide under its belly and up the other side while at full gallop. She remembered a tune he played on his flute, a melody that sounded much sadder than anything he ever admitted feeling.

One thing she knew was that she loved Atiyah— stupidly like in the stories and also in the full glare of day.

She also knew how to find satisfaction in work done well and in the encounters that made the weave of life in a camp. She could make the best of marriage to Raisulu. She would put one foot before the other in the brightness of day. She would not dream, and she would not drop her water jar.

But just as Saffiya carried a sadness, so would she.

There would be no full, night-and-day joy in marriage to Raisulu. To be with him was to be on shifting ground, on quicksand.

Atiyah, the Gift of God. Did he believe he was perfect? No. He pretended, gamely, beautifully trying to live up to his name. And he was so near. She could slip out like a shadow and scramble like a gopher into the guest tent. . . .

Even the thought of it made her shake. If she were caught, she would be brought before the tribe. Her throat would be slit like a camel's, her dishonor washed away in blood.

But what dishonor? There would be no dishonor if she went to tell Atiyah the truth. The semblance of dishonor, that is what she would have to pay for with her life.

If Atiyah would be sad, as she would be sad her whole life, at least let it be a true sadness, not anger, not doubt. Atiyah should know that she had wanted

[ 134 ]

only to go with him, to be his wife as had always been planned.

How could Atiyah doubt her? Atiyah was prideful, and they had been separated for a long time.

Around and around her doubts chased each other. At last, she could bear them no longer. She brushed out her hair and replaited it. She touched her forehead to the ground in a wordless prayer. She slipped out of the tent and hurried across to the guest tent, her heart in her mouth.

Atiyah and Etienne had agreed to keep watch all night.

"Raisulu might send a killer," said Etienne.

"I hope he does," Atiyah answered. "If he comes himself, I'll kill *him!*"

The thought seemed to cheer him.

Halfway through the long night, they both fell into a deep sleep.

Halima found Etienne first in the dark and knew by the strange texture of his hair that he was not Atiyah.

"Excuse me," she said, and stifled a nervous giggle. "I need to find Atiyah."

"Halima!" came Atiyah's voice from the dark.

[ 135 ]

"Good-bye. I'm taking a run," Etienne announced, and rolled out under the wall of the tent.

"No!" Halima said urgently, understanding his misunderstanding. "Stay!" But he was gone.

Atiyah sat bolt upright. He was invisible to Halima, but she knew just where he was. "Go!" he said. "Go now!"

Halima shook her head hard. Her well-planned words had deserted her.

"They'll kill you! Go, Cousin, go, my love, please!" There were tears in Atiyah's voice. Halima heard them, and the hair rose on her arms.

"I have to speak first," said Halima.

"Don't dishonor them," said Atiyah. And then, "Don't dishonor us."

"Honor isn't in what they think I do," said Halima. "Honor is in what I do."

Atiyah caught his breath. Silence filled the tent, and in that silence they heard talking outside.

"Death is in what they think you do," said Atiyah. "Live, Cousin."

"Be quiet, Atiyah!" said Halima. "I *will* go. But I have to tell you something first. After tonight, I'll live in daylight for the tribe. I'll be a wife to the old sheikh, if I must. But in the other true way, in songs

[ 136 ]

and dreams and stories, I will be as we were meant to be, Cousin. That's what I had to tell you."

Halima reached for the edge of the tent, resigned to lifting it, rolling under, creeping silently to her dreary future. She paused, and the moment stretched in darkness. She did not reach to touch Atiyah; she simply savored his presence, wanting to stop time. When she lifted the tent side, a crack of light showed and a foot stomped on her hand. The next moment, there was a woman's voice at the tent entrance, and the smell of coffee.

Etienne walked briskly through the night, trying to clear from his heart a confusion in which he recognized both envy and loneliness. The stars were fading, and a sudden brightness appeared behind the dunes to the east. Daybreak. Already! Etienne walked back toward the gathering of tents and stood watching the goats in the close. The air was cool enough so that their breath made little puffs of steam as they slept.

It occurred to Etienne that he could take his horse and ride away before anyone awoke, and it would not change the happenings of the day by very much. He stood still, watching as the pale dawn light blackened the rectangular tents against the bright-ening sand. The goats began to stir, and back close to the women's tent, he heard the sharp crackle of burning thornbush. He smelled the camel dung as it caught and began to smolder.

He tried to pray that he and Atiyah and Halima would live through the day ahead, but his Christian God, the God of his childhood, seemed hard to reach. The only thought that came to him was that the desert was a good place to die. He smiled to him-self. He was too insignificant to die. Atiyah had told him that he would live to be an old holy man. And his friend seemed to know about such things.

Word of Atiyah's arrival had spread through the tribe. A young man from far away, handsome as a prince, accompanied by a light-faced, blue-eyed Roum!

The black tents were lively with talk, and as soon as the first light streaked the sky, the old men, who slept little, came to sit together outside the guest-tent, in order to be the first to see these guests, to greet and question them.

As Etienne turned back toward the tents, he saw the men gathering and went to them.

"We should wake the other young man and bring him coffee," said one of the elders.

"He will need his sleep, for he traveled far yesterday."

"Let this man tell us about the Roum."

"Is it true, boy, that the Roum warriors cover their bodies with shining metal when they go to battle?"

"And that they sprout feathers from the tops of their heads?"

"And that they never wash?"

Etienne sat down among the old men. As he answered their questions, acting out those things he didn't have words to describe, he saw Saffiya go into the guest tent with coffee. His heart quickened, and for a moment words deserted him as he stared after her. The old men's eyes followed his. When Saffiya came out, Etienne knew by her face that Halima was still inside.

"Our guest is awake now, for Saffiya has brought him coffee," said one old man. "Let us go and greet him."

The man began slowly to rise to his feet. The moment seemed to last forever. Etienne's eyes focused on an extra tent pole leaning against one of the tents, and panic gave way to inspiration.

Etienne jumped to his feet before the elder could move toward the guest tent. "Wait! Let me show you how these Roum warriors prepare for battle!" he shouted with enthusiasm. "Here, some of you warriors line up on this side. Excuse me, Uncle, could you stand just here—that's right! And you three over here, now, you must take part in this, too. Over here . . ."

Soon he had the old men lined up and poised for action, four to each side. Now what? he thought in panic.

"Warriors! Every time I pass, shake your fists in the air and shout, '*Vive le roi! Vive le roi!*' There! Louder! *Vive le roi!* You've got it!"

To the accompaniment of their shouting, Etienne acted out the rowdiest of jousting meets, galloping between the two rows of old men, brandishing the spare tent-pole. The old men shouted at each passing, half in fear, half in merriment. A fool, Etienne thought. I'm a fool for life. But he had their attention.

As he turned back toward the guest tent, he carefully aimed his "lance" at its center supporting pole. He ran at a gallop, singing a French battle song at the top of his lungs. By now the old men were shouting with laughter, the women had come out of their tents to watch, and the children were awake and joining in as well. Clapping and stamping their feet, chanting *"Vive le roi!"* they cheered the clown who had appeared among them.

*CRACK!* Etienne's lance hit the center pole of the guest tent. A rope popped and flew into the air. The tent collapsed in a sky-high cloud of dust, amid shouts and with some help from Saffiya, who seemed to be trying to hold it up on one side.

The noise and hubbub were tremendous, and before calm was restored, Halima was seen coming out of the women's tent, rubbing sleep from her eyes.

"What in the world is going on?" she asked the children. "Is the Roum a djinn? Have we buried our other guest?"

# 22

# Sheikh Raisulu's Feast

The dust had barely settled when men grabbed poles and ropes and raised the guest tent again, drove its pegs deep into the sand, and sent the old men inside to inquire solicitously about the young guest. The smell of roasting coffee beans wafted around the tents. Women poured still-warm beans, rattling, into the carved mortars. Boys wielding pestles almost as tall as themselves threw them down, pounding the beans to powder. The rhythms of their work, reverberating among the hills, invited the Shummari to the guest tent to help their sheikh give hospitality before the wedding ceremony.

Children were sent reluctantly off to tend the herds in the place of their elders. Men washed and prayed with special care, oiled their beards, and donned their cleanest robes. Women painted the soles of their feet red with henna; they opened their coffers and lifted out heavy gold necklaces, which they set gently around each other's necks.

In the kitchen tent, girls heaped platters with bread and dates and dried figs and carried them, two to each side, to the guest tent. Halima and Saffiya helped, with no time to talk and little to say. Sometimes, as they passed each other, their eyes met or their hands clasped briefly.

Only the men could sit inside the tent, but the side was opened and stretched out to new poles to form a breezeway, where women and children could gather. Carpets were hastily brought from other tents and rolled out in this extension. Never had Raisulu received so many, and his people were proud for him. They shouted approval as more poles were brought.

"Roum! Come and help us enlarge this tent!"

"No, Etienne-Roum! Please, stay far from us while we work!"

The story of Etienne's accident was told and en-acted again and again as more people gathered.

The smell of coffee and cardamom, the rich red colors of the carpets exposed to the sun, the red heels of the women and the flashes of gold from their jewels, the laughter and approving excitement of the crowd made Halima's sorrow so out of place that she felt guilty for it. This gathering was for the good of the tribe, and she tried to forget that the occasion for it was her marriage to Sheikh Raisulu.

Coffee dregs piled up outside Raisulu's tent. The men breakfasted, reaching ten at a time for bread from the copper platters, as women threw more dough on the metal bread griddles.

Halima wished that the breakfast would go on forever, but when the sun stood above, she found that all the cups and platters had been gathered up, that the water carriers had made their rounds. The men had washed and were ready for speeches. Her heart sank in dread as Raisulu rose to his feet. She didn't dare even look at Atiyah.

"Shummari," Raisulu began, "People of the Desert, I have brought you here to tell you a story."

Raisulu's people sighed contentedly.

Raisulu's voice ground slowly, spinning out the tale most knew already. "My story begins with a young girl, lost during a storm in the great sand sea, alone and near death. For a day and a night, a night and a day she wandered. Allah, all praise be to Him!, brought her within the reaches of our camp. A huntsman rode forth with his falcon. The prey he found was a treasure far greater than the prey he had sought. He found the young girl and brought her to us, into these very tents where you sit. Slowly, slowly, she recovered from her ordeal, and as she healed, this young woman revealed herself to us in beauty, in skill, and in strength of character."

Raisulu paused and took a deep breath. He looked at Halima for a long moment, silently. Then he turned and spoke to his people.

"This young woman, whom we call Halima, I have asked to become my wife."

A murmur of approval rose from the assembled tribe, as all faces turned to acknowledge Halima.

"A wedding feast is planned for tonight," Raisulu continued. "There will be singing and dancing, feasting, and the giving of the bride-price."

The people cheered with enthusiasm, then quieted, seeing that their sheikh had more to say.

"Into our midst, on this propitious day, have ridden two guests. Listen well, Shummari, for it is up to you to decide how these guests will be treated.

"One guest comes from across the sea. He is called Etienne-Roum. His people have fought for the Christian God. Like us, he is a man of the Book. Unlike us, he is not a builder, but a destroyer, of tents."

At this, the crowd roared with laughter. Raisulu waited until they were quiet.

"Our other guest comes from a people who have been our rivals in the desert, people whom you have fought, worthy and fearsome adversaries. Thanks to the bravery of our warriors, we have some of their best horses and camels: I speak of the Beni Khalid!"

Another roar from the crowd, a mixture of amazement, of indignation, and of excitement.

"But there is more to the story, O Shummari. Bend your ears and attend well."

Not a sound could be heard, even outside the tent, where the women and children sat in rapt attention.

"This son of the Beni Khalid is the first cousin of the woman whom we found lost in the desert, the woman Halima who is to become my bride!"

A buzz of excitement from the crowd, quickly hushed.

Halima stood like stone.

She glimpsed Atiyah, on the other side of Raisulu, suddenly incandescent with hope.

"Tell me, O Shummari, for it will be your decision, how should we receive our guests?"

"Invite them to the wedding!"

"Give them each a camel!"

"*Two* camels for the Destroyer of Tents!"

Sheikh Raisulu held his hands palms out to quiet these suggestions. He cleared his throat and moved into a shaft of sunlight. All eyes were on him. The pulse beat beside his eye.

"I will do more than that, O Shummari," he said at last. "Much more." Raisulu gazed out above the heads of his people, through the tent and the open breezeway, out to the hills of sand and the blue sky. His expression was sad, a little surprised, as if he himself was not sure what he would say next. "I will give up my bride," he said, "whom I have saved from death. In the name of Allah, and of the *'asabiyya,* the code of the desert, which makes all of us as of one tribe, I relinquish the beautiful Halima to her first cousin Atiyah!"

The crowd roared its approval. Men leaped to their feet, fists in the air. Tears streamed down the cheeks of matrons. Halima clutched at a tent pole to keep from falling. Atiyah fell to his knees and kissed Raisulu's hand.

Raisulu raised Atiyah to his feet and then turned again to his people, for there was more to be said.

"Tonight!" he shouted over the tumult, and they quieted. "Tonight, the Beni Shummar will hold a wedding feast surpassing any you have seen, in honor of the wedding of Halima and of her be-trothed, her cousin Atiyah!"

"Allah loves the man who is noble!" shouted

someone in the crowd, and they began a chorus of "Ra-i-sulu, Ra-i-sulu!"

"And what shall we do for the other guest?" someone asked. A hush fell.

"Speak your wish, guest from across the sea."

But Etienne, whose head was still spinning from the turn of events, could think of nothing more in the world that he wished for and no words to express his amazement. As he stood with his mouth open, some jokester shouted, *"Vive le roi!"* The crowd took it up, shouting over and over. Amid the high hilarity that seized them all, Etienne noticed most a flash of Saffiya's gold tooth.

The prayer was read, and the songs were sung. As the day waned and women prepared the roasts and fat-drenched bread, the men raced their finest camels and horses. Raisulu raced among them, his horse kicking up plumes of white sand as he wheeled, raced again, and won, cheered on by his people.

The night rang with music and merriment, and the young men danced, each resting an arm on his neighbor's shoulder, all eyes on the stamp of their feet as, faster and faster, they followed the beat of the drum.

Atiyah and Halima withdrew to the bridal tent, which Saffiya had lovingly prepared.

Etienne joined the bachelor's dance, keeping time to the goatskin drum with the kicking of his heels.

In the morning a messenger was sent to the Beni Khalid, to the Wadi Hammamat, where Atiyah knew Essafeh would likely still be camped with his people. Halima, Atiyah, and Etienne were escorted into the desert, with fine gifts from Raisulu and Saffiya, a herd of camels necklaced in blue, and ample provisions. For five days they rode across the desert with banners flying.

When the outlying herdsmen of the Wadi Hammamat brought word of their approach, the women of the Beni Khalid let down their long black hair and sang out loud trills of welcome and the men rode forth to meet them. Nazreen, riding on the neck of her father's camel, flew like a hawk to greet her sister.

From that day to this, the legend grew—how Essafeh sent gifts to Raisulu of the Shummari and begged his visit, and how the two tribes lived in peace and friendship—and when the story is told at night in the tents of hair, the storyteller will often add:

*"They had peace and plenty, year after year.*
*May God send such fortune to you who sit here."*

In later years, Atiyah made his peace with Saladeen and, as sheikh of the Beni Khalid, sent one of Halima's younger brothers to ride at the right hand of the caliph Abu Yacub in his triumphal march between Fez and Tlemcen. This brother, a tough and wily warrior, fought in battles as far away as Spain for the Marinid Empire, to extend Islam among the heathen. But Atiyah and Halima never left the desert, because it pleased them to stay there, among their sons and daughters.